Weekend with Her Bachelor

Weekend with Her Bachelor

The Bachelor Auction Returns

Jeannie Moon

TULE
PUBLISHING

Dedication

To my friend and mentor, Jane Porter.
Thank you for giving me a place to call home.

Prologue

Eighteen Months Earlier

GAVIN CLARK HATED surprises. When he was six years old, his friend Nick Palotay jumped out of the classroom coat closet and scared Gavin so bad he peed himself. It was not a great way to start first grade, and Nick had never let him live it down.

Ever since then, he made it a point to be prepared for anything. And it didn't matter if it was school, his job, or even sports. Gavin worked out harder, studied longer, and pushed himself to be the best. So, even though his job as an ER physician at busy Bozeman Hospital threw him something unexpected every day, he'd prepared so well, nothing spooked him.

"I really hate it when winter doesn't respect her damn boundaries." Gavin donned a heavy parka as he and the response team rode the elevator to the roof. A LifeFlight was heading in with a patient. The sudden, severe October snowstorm had made roads treacherous, and he figured the person on the helicopter had been in a crash. "Do we know what we have?"

The nurse with him looked at the chart. "Teenage boy, head and neck injury. He wasn't responsive."

"Where is he coming in from?"

The nurse hesitated for a second. "Marietta."

As soon as he heard his hometown's name, Gavin's stomach lurched. It was going to be someone he knew, no doubt there; Marietta was the kind of place where everyone knew everyone. "Why didn't they take him to Marietta Regional?"

"The only way out of campus was blocked because of a multi-car crash. The roads are treacherous; people are spinning out all over the place. Airlifting him was the best option, but the local hospital has no landing pad. Everything conspired against them."

"Shit." All Gavin could think was that precious minutes were lost flying the kid to Bozeman. He understood the logistics, but it could have cost them the time they needed.

They heard the sound of the rotors cutting through the cold night air, and the landing lights illuminated the spot where the helicopter touched down.

"Let's go!" Gavin yelled, hauling the stretcher next to him. "I need his status."

The flight nurse began reading off the patient's condition as soon as the door opened, shouting as the rotors powered down. "Sixteen-year-old male, severe head trauma. He took a nasty hit on the football field. Non-responsive. He's intubated and we've been doing chest compressions for a few minutes."

Jesus. Chest compressions? The sad look in the nurse's eyes told him the patient was already gone. The anguished cries he heard from behind her told him there was a mother who was coming to that same conclusion.

Gavin took in the uniform as they transferred the patient onto the stretcher. He remembered his years playing for the Grizzlies, and how much it meant to him. When his eyes reached the player's face, Gavin's heart jumped to his throat.

"Oh, my God." It was Troy Downey. Coach's grandson.

Gavin looked at the motionless form and a wave of memories hit him like a ton of bricks. In his mind's eye, he saw Troy, maybe four years old, running across the field with a football. He could barely keep hold of it in his little hands, but he kept running down the field like he was playing in the championship game. Troy might have been four years old when Gavin made varsity. But age had nothing to do with his spirit. The little pipsqueak loved the game. He loved being around the team, and he was adopted like an unofficial mascot.

Gavin was frozen. He was thinking about the boy he used to know, and about all the potential that had been snuffed out in a moment.

The gurney jerked forward and the trauma team headed for the elevator with Troy. Gavin stood there, the wind and snow blowing around him, until one of the nurses finally laid a hand on his arm. "Dr. Clark? Gavin?"

"I know him," Gavin said, fighting the emotion. "I've known him since he was little."

Her voice was gentle, quiet. "Unfortunately, the longer you're in this job, the more of them you'll know. Let's get inside. Maybe you can help him."

Moving with her toward the team, he could only imagine what Coach and his family were going through. Troy was a good kid, and from what Gavin had heard, he was destined for a great future.

Now, though, that seemed impossible.

Gavin steadied his nerves and reminded himself that this was what he'd been trained for. The years in school, the long hours, the lack of a life… had led him to a place where he could help people.

Maybe he could help Troy Downey.

Chapter One

ALLY BEAUMONT STARED at the guest list and quietly cursed under her breath.

She knew there was a possibility her asshole of an ex-boyfriend would be at the destination wedding she'd been planning for a close friend, but she had no idea he was one of the groomsmen, and that he was going to be one of her main contacts during the festivities. Since when had he and the groom gotten that close?

A fun event had turned into something she was now dreading, putting Ally on a luxury ranch weekend with the man who had jilted her two days before their wedding, and no date of her own. She'd been informed that Lars, her ex, was bringing his lady friend for the weekend. She was his soulmate, apparently, and he had never been happier.

Bastard.

But Lars in the mix or not, her focus had to be on the bride and groom, and her goal was always to make the weekend special for everyone attending the wedding. Even her asshole of an ex. The venue was perfection. She stared at the pictures of the ranch pinned to the project board in her office. She couldn't stop looking, and considering the view from her office window consisted of Puget Sound, with Bainbridge Island in the distance, that really said something.

The truth was, as much as Ally enjoyed her life in Seattle, she was still in love with her home state of Montana. And she knew the beauty and vastness of the Whispering River Ranch, set in the western mountains, was going to blow the guests away. There was nothing like a Montana spring.

"Ally?" Turning to the door of her office, her assistant nodded to the phone. "It's a woman named Lisa Barnes. She said you know her from home. Something about an auction?"

Lisa Barnes. Wow. She hadn't seen her in years. Lisa was one of her best friends at Marietta High School, and the two of them used to hide in the corner of the library, dreaming about finding Prince Charming. "Hey!" she said when she picked up the phone. "Fancy hearing from you! I saw your name on the wedding guest list…"

"Yup. Wedding. I can't make it, unfortunately. Work. But tell me you're coming home next week before you head out for that ranch." Lisa was straight to the point and blunt as always.

"Hello to you too!" Ally said sarcastically. "I was planning on two weeks at home before I went to the mountains. I want to see my parents and catch up around town. What's this you mentioned about an auction?"

"The second annual Marietta Bachelor Auction."

"Wait… a bachelor auction?" Why the hell was she calling about a bachelor auction?

"It's a fundraiser for the hospital. They're raising money for a rooftop helipad. We've had them before, they stage it at Grey's, lots of fun, but I thought you'd like to know that this round of bachelors went to school with us."

"Who?" There were some fine looking boys back in school with her. One in particular she still thought about.

"Code Matthews, Nick Palotay, Colt Ewing—"

"Whoa." Those *were* some gorgeous men going up on the auction block. "I bet there's been a run on the bank."

"You could say that, but there's one more. *Doctor* Gavin Clark."

Gavin. Clark. "R-really?" Gavin Clark was at the root of all her teen angst. He was her first crush, her first dance, her first kiss. Gavin was her first everything. It was quite possible, based on the way her heartbeat picked up, that she never got over him. He was sweet and handsome. A nice guy of the highest order—and of course, she'd managed to hurt him because she was stupid.

"He's going up for auction? I'm confused." Ally was definitely confused. "Gavin didn't like to draw attention to himself. That doesn't sound like his kind of gig."

"Last year, Coach Downey's grandson was killed in an on field collision. You had to have heard about that, you babysat him, didn't you?"

"I did. Broke my heart when my mom told me. He was

such a good kid." Troy *was* a good kid, too. Whenever she ran into him in town, he was polite and sweet as could be. It was a tragic, tragic loss for the whole community.

"The roads were blocked, and he had to be airlifted to Bozeman because Marietta General doesn't have a helipad. The guys were devoted to Coach. When he asked them to participate in the event, to raise money for the helipad, they were all in."

That didn't surprise her. They might have been hell raisers, but all four of them were good guys. For a moment, Ally wished she had a matchmaking business; those four hunky men would make her a fortune, and make some women very happy.

But Gavin was the one who set her heart racing. "My mom told me he'd gone to medical school."

"He's an emergency physician," Lisa sighed. "Apparently, he's up for anything regarding a date. Can you imagine?"

"Hmm." She could imagine. She could imagine it very well. An idea started to form in Ally's head. Maybe Gavin would be up for a weekend with her. At a wedding. "Do the bids go very high?"

"Sometimes a few thousand dollars. Although, word on the street is the guys opened up the dates to allow for some flexibility because they want to pull in some big money. What are you thinking?"

She was thinking she might have a date to the wedding, after all. Buying herself a big, handsome cowboy-doctor was very appealing. And Ally could afford it. Hell, her business just cracked the seven-figure mark, but even if it hadn't, she could sell the engagement ring Lars left her with and have a grand old time helping out Marietta. That wasn't a bad idea, actually. He'd been hinting that he wanted the ring back. What better way to give it back to him than by bringing a sweet, brilliant, handsome man to the wedding.

"So are you coming? I'd love to see you. I've missed you the last few times you've been in town."

"You bet," Ally proclaimed. "It's a good cause."

"Yay! I can't wait to see you! Vivi is coming too. It's been too long."

Ally smiled. She, Lisa, and Vivi Walker were inseparable in high school. They each went their separate ways for college, but kept in touch through social media and email, getting together at odd times. The auction at Grey's was going to be a fun reunion. And if she won Gavin Clark in the auction, she'd consider the trip home an epic win.

Opening her desk drawer, Ally pulled out the velvet box that held the custom-made diamond ring that Lars had given her two years ago. The stone was flawless and it was massive, having been appraised at over thirty thousand dollars. She had a friend in downtown Seattle who owned an estate jewelry store who'd offered to take the ring off her hands whenever she was ready to unload it.

Gazing out at the ferries crossing Puget Sound, Ally decided it was time to make a phone call. The big, fat diamond was going to get her a wedding date.

FAMILY DINNERS AT the Clark Ranch were noisy and chaotic. There was always a friend at the table, along with family, and no one ever left hungry. Gavin tried to get home at least once a week, because aside from missing his parents and his brothers, he wanted to fill up on his mother's stews, fried chicken, mashed potatoes, and home baked biscuits and pies. He wasn't the least bit ashamed of wanting to see his family, or for wanting to eat.

He enjoyed the hard physical work of ranch life, and as stressful as his life in the ER was, he could expend more energy in two hours in the barn than he would in a full day at the hospital.

What he did was serious, Gavin knew that, and important, but the land was in his blood. His family had been on this patch of acreage for almost two hundred years—a few members of his family were driven from England for being sympathetic to the Scots during the rising in 1746. Eventually, after fighting their way through several wars on the East Coast, the Clarks found their way to Montana.

"Ma," he said though the bite of food he was still chewing. "This is the best meal I've had in ages."

"You mean since the one you had here last week?" His mother grinned.

"That's a long time when you're hungry." Gavin survived

on takeout and frozen food when he was living in Bozeman. He loved the work, but didn't love life in the city. He couldn't imagine how people survived in really congested places like LA or New York. Yet a lot of people his age were doing just that.

Maybe the fact that he didn't want to brave the big city made him unsophisticated, but he liked space. His idea of a workout was training a difficult horse, fixing a fence, or throwing hay bales.

A pickup game of football with his brothers and a couple of beers at Grey's after was his idea of a good time.

Simple. Unsophisticated. Yeah, that was him. *Doctor Hayseed* as he was called by a few at work.

Of the five Clark brothers, Gavin was in the middle. Eli and Dan were older, while Jonah was five years behind him. Luke, the youngest, had just turned twenty-three and was serving his country overseas in the Marine Corps.

Eli was the only one married, and he and his wife were expecting the first grandchild. The only one who hadn't embraced ranch life at all, his brother was a lawyer living in Minneapolis. Their parents hadn't liked losing their oldest child to the city, but he wasn't that far away and he was happy. That was all his folks really wanted.

Dan sat next to him and gave him a quick elbow jab. "So me and the boys will be down at Grey's tomorrow to watch you auction yourself off to the masses tomorrow. I hear many lovely Marietta ladies have broken into their piggy banks to bid on the group of you."

Gavin still didn't love the idea of the auction, but he'd do anything for Coach D, and having been the one who was there when Troy died, who signed the death certificate, he really had no choice but to do his part.

"If it brings the helipad to the hospital, I don't care. The minutes lost getting Troy to Bozeman might have saved him."

After that night, Gavin dove into his work with a vengeance. Taking extra shifts and learning all he could about Traumatic Head Injuries, as well as collision injuries like Troy's, he'd vowed nothing like that would happen again on his watch. Not without his best effort. Gavin knew, intellectually, that he wasn't responsible for Troy's death, but he still felt guilty for not saving the kid. He felt like he let his coach, Troy's family, and the whole community down.

"It's a good thing you're doing, son." His father wasn't much for showmanship, but even Ben Clark understood where it was coming from. "Besides," he said to Dan and Jonah, "I don't see you boys doing your part for the Coach."

Gavin raised an eyebrow. "That's because they're both ugly. You drop them or something, Ma?"

"The three of you can stop now," his mother chided. "I'm sure you boys will raise a lot of money for the hospital."

He hoped so. It would be the only consolation for having to put himself through the humiliation of being sold off like a prize stallion.

"I don't mean to rub this in," Dan said quietly. "But I hear Jenny Gaston is gearing up to bid on you *big*."

Gavin groaned. He never liked to talk unkindly about any woman, but Jenny had been a thorn in his side since high school. Pretty in a very obvious way, she thought because her daddy had ranching money, she had a right to do whatever she wanted, including telling lies about people when it suited her needs.

He'd found out she was the reason Ally had cut him off. Jenny had been after him for the better part of the last fifteen years, going back as far as their second year of high school. And while he wasn't sure what went down, exactly, he knew she was at the center of his fallout with Ally. The story Jenny told was all bullshit, but if Ally wasn't willing to listen to reason, if she was going to believe the lies, there was nothing he could do about it.

There had to be some kind of sickness associated with Jenny's obsession, but Gavin was hard pressed to put his finger on it. He'd been a target of hers for a long time, and it looked like nothing had changed.

"Maybe she's moved on," he said hopefully.

Dan chuckled. "Think again."

"Shit." Gavin regretted it the minute he said it, just like he regretted asking Jenny to dance at a school party. It happened once. They were both fifteen at the time.

"Language, Gavin…" His mother had no tolerance for strong language in her presence, even from her adult sons.

Finishing his meal, he excused himself to do some chores in the barn. He was hoping he could clear his head, and get his nerves under control. Good, hard physical work always seemed to do the trick. The April air still took on a chill at night, so he wanted to make sure all the horses had blankets and plenty of bedding.

He was giving some attention to a just foaled mare when he heard footsteps. If he had to guess, it was a couple of his friends, if not all of them. None of them were too happy about the auction. It just wasn't something they'd have done. If ever the phrase 'take one for the team' applied, this was it. Because when Coach asked, there wasn't a chance they were saying no.

"Are either of you nervous? I'm nervous." Nick Palotay sat on a farrier's stool that was in the aisle, and Colt Ewing leaned into the wall.

"This sucks," Colt said. "I heard it's going to be packed. Desperate women all waiting to bid on us. A fucking nightmare."

"For a good cause," Gavin added. "A very good cause. And you don't know that they're all desperate." Jenny was desperate. And crazy.

"What do you have to wear?" Nick wondered. "My sister has been on my ass about every detail. She's trying to make me look like a magazine ad."

"I have a very expensive suit. I can thank Rowan for that," he grumbled. "I think I've only worn a suit ten times

WEEKEND WITH HER BACHELOR

in my life—on job interviews, to a couple of weddings and a funeral. I wear jeans or scrubs." Gavin didn't know what to expect, but he'd heard the same as the other guys—that Grey's would be standing room only. Good for the fundraiser, bad for his ability to walk through town without getting shit for being a pretty boy.

"If we don't raise a butt load of money, we're never going to hear the end of it," Colt added.

That was another shitty truth. The four of them had led their high school football team to the state championship. It gave them some minor local celebrity status, and brought the same amount of scorn from those in town who had dubbed them "entitled".

The three of them settled into silence, the only sound came from the horses in their stalls, settling in for the night. That was until his mother came into the barn and gave them a good once over.

"My goodness. The three of you look like your best horse died. Why the long faces?"

Colt and Nick tipped their hats to his mother.

"Evening, Miz Clark," Colt said. "We were just talking about the auction. It's got us all a bit on edge."

"You're all going to be fine. Stop worrying about the darn auction, and have some fun with it."

Christine Clark was the perfect rancher's wife; a mix of sweetness and toughness, she handled her men like a pro. Taking no bull from any of them, she kept their lives on track, raising her sons to be good, responsible men. And while she kept a beautiful home, with her husband she also managed a successful business. "Now, why don't you boys come to the porch? I made a cake. It's chocolate."

Without another word, she turned, leaving the barn and the three men with a directive. Gavin chuckled. He guessed they were having cake.

Nick rose from the stool. "I never turn down your mother's cake."

Colt grinned and pushed off the wall. "Yeah, me either."

Colt had spent a lot of time sleeping on the floor of Gavin's room when they were growing up. Living with his uncle had been hell and the Clarks always made a place for him whenever he needed it.

Gavin stroked the nose of his favorite mare and moved to his friends.

Nick shrugged. "I wish I knew what we were in for. The only good thing is that I didn't keep the date open-ended. Not like you idiots."

"Yeah. That was a mistake," Gavin agreed as they exited the barn. "But we're in it now, and I'm not going to say anything that might make Coach or his family feel bad. I just hate surprises."

"Yeah." Nick slapped him on the back, chuckling. "I remember."

Chapter Two

S HE'D NEVER SEEN Grey's so crowded.

Ally hadn't been home very much since she graduated from college and moved to Seattle, but she'd never seen the popular watering hole this crowded. But based on the way Lisa had talked about the auction, she imagined people had come from neighboring towns to be part of the event.

Earlier, as she walked through Marietta, she loved how the place hadn't changed. It was a little harder to find a place to park, but overall, the warm brick buildings lining Main Street and the familiar family owned shops made her think about the years spent growing up in a place like this.

Everyone was connected. Even people who didn't know each other that well, and there were some, considered one another neighbors and friends. Newbies to town always remarked on the friendliness, the neighborliness, of the residents. It was hard to feel lonely in a place like Marietta, and for that reason alone Ally had missed it.

Seattle was a friendly city, and she had a group of friends and her business, but it wasn't like here. When she walked into Grey's tonight, she'd been greeted by at least twenty people, and she was sure at least half of them didn't recognize her. The other half couldn't believe how much she'd changed.

Finding Lisa and Vivi in the crowd wasn't easy, but giving the room a slow turn, she finally saw them in the second tier of tables. They were close enough to the stage to see, but not so close that the bachelors would be able to get a clear look at who was bidding. She hoped they couldn't. She wasn't all too certain how Gavin was going to feel about her bidding on him. The two of them hadn't parted on great terms, and most of that was her fault, but she was counting on one thing: that his willingness to raise money for the hospital outweighed his animosity towards her. Then again, he may have forgotten all about their little falling out.

Nah. She'd never have that kind of luck.

Stopping at the bar, she saw Rowan Palotay, another longtime friend, and grabbed her arm as she walked by. "Hey!"

"Oh my GOD!" Rowan squealed. "Ally! I can't believe you're here!

"I am! I can't believe how packed this place is. It looks like there's going to be some hardcore bidding."

"I hope so. We've worked really hard on this event. We have a bet going with Lily Taylor that we'll raise more money than she did at last year's auction. But you! You look amazing, Ally. Are you going to bid?"

"Ah, maybe." Ally knew how close Rowan was to her

brother, and Nick was one of Gavin's best friends. Best she kept her plans to herself.

"Well, your favorite tight end is number four out of the gate." They used to joke about how Gavin's position on the team was descriptive of one of his best attributes. "He's looking fine, if I do say so myself."

"I'm sure they all look great. That was never their problem."

"Nope. Never was. Look, I have to go, but we'll talk later." Rowan gave her a quick hug. "Eeep! I'm so glad to see you!"

Rowan dashed off, and Ally weaved through the crowd, settling herself in a chair between Lisa and Vivi. "Together again!" Vivi cried, as she threw her arms around Ally. The three of them hadn't been together in the same place in over five years. They just couldn't get their schedules to align. So, even if she didn't end up with the winning bid, Ally was glad that she'd come home to see her friends. It had been too long.

"So, are we bidding? Who are we bidding on?" Vivi asked, sipping her drink through a tiny straw.

Vivi, with her boundless enthusiasm and big personality, was going to exhaust them before the night was over. Her friend, a freelance assistant, kept the lives of very busy people organized, and she was doing well enough to buy an apartment for herself in one of the prettiest areas in Chicago. Fantastic as it was, Ally didn't know how she kept her energy up.

"So, Lisa told me you might be bidding on Gavin," Vivi wondered. "That's brave after what happened."

"Nothing happened."

"Sure it did."

"No, it didn't."

"Did…" Vivi teased.

"Stop. I'm not doing this."

"Hmmpf," Vivi snuffled before going back to her drink. "Did."

Ally pinched the bridge of her nose in frustration. She spoke the truth, regardless of what her friend thought. To her great regret, nothing had ever happened between her and Gavin, save one very slow, sweet, perfect kiss the night before he left for college.

"We're still the geeks," Lisa said as she scanned the room. "Look at the crowd of A-listers rolling in here. I even heard Hayley is back in town." Hayley Dawn O'Malley had gone to school with them, but left town right after graduation to make a name for herself in Hollywood. The combination of talent, looks, and brains proved unstoppable, turning Hayley into a bona fide movie star.

Ally also remembered her as being very sweet. "Didn't her grandma just pass?" Ally asked, hoping to redirect the conversation. "My mom filled me in. Says Hayley's been working at the old house."

Truthfully, Ally couldn't care less about what people

thought about her. Neither should Lisa, who was five-ten, well educated, a successful lawyer, and stunning to boot. High school was a long time ago, and people changed. Hell, Ally had changed. A lot.

Done with thinking, or in this case over-thinking, it was time for a drink. "Hey, Mardie?" Ally flagged down the waitress and ordered a glass of white wine. She wished she could order a really big glass of white wine, like an extra-large coffee, but that might sound desperate. *Can I have an extra-large Pinot Grigio? You know, super-sized? You only have one size?* Damn.

"Anything else, ladies?" Mardie tilted her head at Vivi and Lisa, whose glasses were empty. And any empty glass at Grey's was unacceptable.

"Bring them another round," Ally said before they responded. If the three of them were going to have a good time in this madhouse, they'd need all the help they could get. The bar was electric, but Ally had to admit her own personal rush was being fueled by the money she had sitting in a bank account in Seattle, just waiting to be spent.

This was, without a doubt, the craziest thing she'd ever done. Allison Beaumont didn't take stupid risks with money. She was practical, thorough, but never reckless, and this was pretty reckless. She could just donate the money. There were two or three charities, including the Marietta fundraiser, that could benefit from Lars's tremendous ego. And that's all the ring was. He hadn't listened to Ally's preferences for size or cut, he just went out and bought a big ring. Bigger meant better.

It was the beginning of the end for them.

In the long run, Lars dumping her just days before their wedding wasn't a bad thing. Ally had seen the marriages that were built around excess and self-absorption unravel. It happened more often than not. Everything appeared perfect, until it wasn't. The imperfection eventually took over the relationships, seeping out one drop at a time. Couples who relished the small things in life, the flaws and challenges, did a lot better in the long run.

That's what Ally was holding out for, and looking back, she hoped that she would have walked away from Lars on her own before it was too late. But who knows. She was blinded by the white dress.

It had been over a year since her life fell apart. But she'd pushed forward, giving everything she had to other couples looking for a happy ever after. Her business took off like a rocket.

Mardie delivered their drinks and before Ally realized it, she was downing another. Liquid courage, her mother always called it.

The bar was standing room only. Looking around at the folks gathered for the event, she could see by the way everyone was talking to Coach Downey and his wife that this was more than social. This was support, and it was the thing she missed most about her home.

Ally glanced up to see the four bachelors looking down at the crowd from the landing above the main room. Damn they were hot, and each in their own way. But Gavin? There was something about him—strong, quiet, brilliant—the man had it all, and it was nicely wrapped up in a dark-haired, hazel-eyed, six-foot-four-inch package of gorgeousness.

There was a squeal from a table near the stage, and Ally saw Mandy Pryce and her mean-girl friends looking over the program and then glancing up at the landing. Jenny Gaston was with them, but she wasn't looking at the guys. No, her wicked baby blues were trained right on Ally. Honestly, considering the trouble she caused, Ally was surprised Jenny even made eye contact. But always having more nerve than conscience, Jenny was behaving as she always had—like an entitled brat. She lied and manipulated people to get close to Gavin, and Jenny didn't care who was hurt in the process.

Looking up at the guys one more time, Gavin was surveying the crowd, and Ally's breath caught just taking him in. He was thirty-one to her twenty-nine, and once upon a time she'd dreamed of being with him forever.

Gavin had that effect on women. He was probably doing it right now, without even knowing it, casting his spell over the crowd. Ally—practical, focused Ally—was falling deep into the romantic well. Just looking at Gavin made her ache.

Some things never changed.

Without warning, Gavin turned his head and his eyes locked on hers. He froze. She could see his posture go rigid right where he stood. His face, stony and hard to read, made Ally reconsider her entire plan.

The last thing she needed was an angry cowboy on her hands.

No. She couldn't second guess herself.

Ally needed him, and there was no one else she could trust to play a convincing boyfriend, while keeping things platonic between them.

He was still staring at her, and in the excitement of the moment, she smiled at him. She couldn't help it.

The problem was he didn't smile back.

"SHIT," GAVIN MUTTERED.

Code Matthews looked over the rail and Gavin saw him scanning the crowd. "What?" Code asked. "Is crazy Mandy looking up here? She was scoping out Palotay earlier. And Jenny is here. You knew that, right?"

He'd seen Jenny; and he'd found out she intended to bid on him, just as his brother said.

Damn. "No. Not Mandy. It's…it's nothing. There are just a lot of people here."

One person in particular, though, had his attention. She looked different, but there was no doubt the redhead sitting near the stage was Ally Beaumont. When she flashed her million-dollar smile up at him, Gavin was eighteen again.

What the hell was she doing here? The last he heard, she

was running an event planning business in Seattle and she was engaged. His mother made sure to fill him in on that news; the guy's name was Sven or Jan or some such shit like that.

Gazing down while she looked up, Gavin's heart pounded. Women had come and gone in his life, but none ever stuck. In the back of his mind, he always secretly compared them with Ally. Never had anyone else been his friend, someone he could tell anything to. Maybe that made him a candy ass, but to him a woman was more than a warm body.

Ally had always been more than that.

"Okay," Code said. "So the redhead who's looking up this way is *hot*. Do you know her? She looks familiar."

Gavin kept his eyes fixed. "It's Ally Beaumont."

He knew the silence from his friend was shock. In high school, Ally was the wallflower. The geeky girl who wasn't petite and perky. Instead of being a cheerleader, she was in the band. Instead of going out on a Saturday night, she stayed home and read books. She was funny, and sweet, and there were times he'd have rather been with her than his boys.

But in true high school fashion, the mean girls got involved and preyed on Ally's insecurities, making her second guess their friendship. She might have thought he considered her a pity case back then, but he didn't. Gavin really liked her, and just when he thought they might have a chance for something more, she let him down in the worst possible way.

He hadn't ever considered having to see her again.

But there she was, and while he had no idea what she was planning, the look on her gorgeous face told him she meant business.

"I don't remember Ally being so… uh…" Code didn't know what to say. "She's *really* hot."

"Yeah. I need some air," Gavin groaned.

"Air?" Rowan was behind him, hands on her hips. "Oh, no. You're going to run for it."

"Don't be ridiculous—"

"Go! In there!" She pointed to the storage room where the food and beer had been set up. "There's a window in there. But don't even think about jumping and making a getaway. I will find you."

"Jump? Are you nuts? I'm not jumping, Ro."

"I don't put anything past the lot of you." With those words, she stormed off.

Colt looked straight at Nick. "Your sister is nuts."

"This isn't news to me. Just don't get her mad or I'll hear about it forever."

"Come on, Cody," Mrs. D said. "Let's go."

"First. Effing perfect," Code mumbled, heading down the stairs with Mrs. Downey. All Gavin could think was that it was like a dead man walking. The hoots and catcalls started before his friend even hit the stage.

This was going to be a long, long night.

WEEKEND WITH HER BACHELOR

ALLY WAS GETTING nervous; some serious money had been tossed around tonight, and she just wasn't used to being in the spotlight. Her bid, if she threw the whole thing on the pile of money already raised, would be the most forward, bold, and garish thing she'd ever done.

It could backfire in a big way. But it would get her a date. Gavin's offering in the program was simple and direct. *"Your wish is my command..."*

It was also complete crap.

"There's no way he wrote this," Ally said pointing at the program. Lisa and Vivi looked at the blurb and each raised a well-groomed eyebrow.

Ally shook her head. "No way. Gavin would never give up that much control. It's not in his nature."

"Who do you think is responsible?" Vivi wondered.

"Probably one of the organizers. They mean well, but seriously? This will definitely bring out all the crazies." Crazies like Jenny.

She had no choice now. Ally had to save him.

"With that kind of promise, I might bid on him," Vivi said under her breath.

However, once Ally, who'd felt a cold wave of anger wash through her body, locked her gaze on her friend, Vivi put her hands up in retreat.

"Kidding. Kidding. Wow."

"And now for our last bachelor of the night, I give you Doctor Gavin Clark!" Coach was really enjoying his role as emcee, his voice booming, and she had to give credit—the guys were doing their best to play to the crowd of liquored-up women.

Gavin stepped onto the stage, escorted by Mrs. D, and when the lights came up, he couldn't help but be who he was. Clad in an expensive dark gray suit with a lighter gray shirt open at the collar, Gavin tugged at his cuffs before flashing a devastating grin. Confident and sexy, without the cocky edge, there was a collective gasp as every ovary in the place exploded.

Ally's sure did. Every emotion, every desire attached to Gavin flashed and burned. She ached watching him walk to the front of the stage, stopping and motioning for the crowd to bring it when it was time for the bidding.

"Gavin is an emergency physician in Bozeman, but he grew up right here on his parents' ranch. An expert horseman, he was the tight end…"

Squeals of delight came up from the crowd. "I'LL BET HE HAS A TIGHT END!" someone shouted.

Coach waved his hand. "Keep it clean, ladies. He's up for pretty much anything on his date with the winning bidder as long as it's legal. So that leaves *lots* of possibilities. I'd like to start the bidding at five hundred dollars."

Mandy's hand shot up before Coach could take a breath. "Thank you for starting us off, Mandy."

Gavin looked stricken at the bid.

"Six do I hear… there we have six hundred? Seven hundred? Eight hundred." The bids were creeping up, but no one had blown away the field like with the other bachelors.

"Twenty-five hundred dollars!" came a voice from the end of the bar.

Craning her neck, Ally wasn't really surprised when she got a look at the bidder. There was Jenny, her finger sliding up and down the stem of a wine glass. Cool, casual, arrogant, as always, Gavin's eyes went wide, and for the first time since he came on stage, he looked in Ally's direction. Did he want her to bid?

Winning Gavin in the auction had been her plan, that hadn't changed. But there was no denying she would get some perverse pleasure out of winning a bidding war with the woman who'd messed up their relationship. Time for her to jump in. The town was always looking for something to talk about.

"Five thousand." Ally raised her hand slowly, and Gavin's expression stilled.

"Well, thank you, young lady. We have a bid of five thousand dollars. Do I hear five thousand-five hundred?"

"Ten thousand," came Jenny's response.

Ooohs and ahhs rose from the crowd.

"That's an insane amount of money," Lisa whispered.

It was, but now she was getting pissed. Ally was competitive. No one was going to win this bachelor without a fight. Especially Jenny.

"I have ten thousand dollars, do I have eleven thousand?

Ten thousand going once…"

"Twelve thousand," Ally said.

"Thirteen." Jenny walked to the edge of the stage and glared at Ally.

Glancing up, Ally actually felt for Gavin a little. Bids had never gone this high. He must have felt like a prize racehorse.

It wasn't going to stop her, but she did feel for him.

"Fifteen thousand," Ally said casually.

"Eighteen thousand," came Jenny's next bid.

"Well this is unexpected! Ladies? I have a bid of eighteen *thousand* dollars. Do I hear nineteen? Nineteen? No? Eighteen going once, twice…"

This was getting stupid.

"Twenty-five thousand dollars." Ally called out. Turning, she saw her opponent in the bidding war freeze. Jenny's eyes, cold and stark, conveyed her anger. She'd been beaten. With a glance over her shoulder and a wave of her hand, Jenny indicated she was out.

"Twenty-five thousand dollars! Ladies, that's remarkable. Any more? Are we done? Twenty-five thousand going once… going twice… and…"

Not intimidated, Ally was ready to stare Jenny down, just in case she decided to make one more bid, only to see her very angry daddy had joined her at the end of the bar. Apparently, the Bank of Daddy had cut off her credit.

"And SOLD—" the gavel cracked down, "—to the young lady for twenty-five thousand dollars! We have exceeded our fundraising goal, ladies and gentlemen! Thank you, darlin'." Coach reached down from the stage and shook her hand. "That's very, very generous of you. You've bought yourself a doctor."

Everyone in the bar stood up and clapped for her. There were cheers and whistles, and Ally couldn't tell if it was appreciation for the donation or for beating Jenny Gaston. It might have been a little of both.

Thank you, Lars, she thought. *Your ring went for a good cause.*

She'd won. She'd actually won. Ally didn't know if she'd even have the nerve to make the bid, knowing it would draw so much attention to her. And now she'd done it, and beaten one of the mean girls at her own game.

But then, as the adrenaline dropped off, giving Ally the chance to think about what had just happened, she felt a little sick.

Chapter Three

THE BUZZ HADN'T stopped and the room felt as if it were closing in on her. Bolting to the door that led to the street, Ally walked in a few quick circles before she bent over, grasping her midsection. She prayed she didn't throw up.

What the hell had she done? She'd just spent twenty-five thousand dollars on a *person*.

"That was obscene," came the deep male voice. It didn't take him long to find her. "I mean, I'm glad Jenny didn't win, but twenty-five grand?"

"I don't need you lecturing me, Gavin. You should be happy. You brought in the biggest bid."

"I'm not lecturing you, but I feel like a piece of meat. That's a lot of money, Ally. What made you bid like that?"

"I wanted to win." *I wanted to win you.*

She hadn't faced him yet. She couldn't, but he wasn't having any of it. She felt Gavin's hands on her shoulders, and gently he turned her around.

Seeing him at a distance affected Ally because the memories welled up inside her, but up close? Gavin's presence was overwhelming, and it was more than nostalgia—this was want. Pure and simple. Their past coupled with his physical presence was a powerful mix. She wanted him, and Ally couldn't ever remember having such a visceral reaction to a man.

It was the difference between who they were and who they'd become. The last time she'd spoken to Gavin, he was just twenty. Ally was still a teenage girl. So much had changed.

He was better looking that even she remembered. But of course, his age played a factor—he'd grown into himself. Gone was the lanky boy she remembered; instead, a broad, muscular man had replaced him. He'd grown up on a farm, raising and riding quarter horses, but from where she stood, Gavin would fit in with the most successful business people she knew. Confident, professional, he wore his suit like an extension of himself. There was a bit of scruff across his angular jaw, and instead of keeping his dark hair cropped close as he did when he was younger, it was a little longer. Wavy and dark, she just wanted to touch it…

"Ally?"

Oh, God. He was talking to her. "Yeah, sorry. I zoned."

"Can you cover the bid?"

"Excuse me?" He did not just ask her that. Good grief. "Of course I can cover the bid. What kind of question is that?"

"I didn't mean to offend you—"

"Well, you did. Congratulations. Even if I hadn't gotten an unexpected windfall, I could have made a five-figure donation. No problem. Sheesh."

"Okay, sorry. That was out of line." He shuffled his feet nervously. "What windfall?"

Ally sighed, shrugged. "I was engaged, and last year, two days before my wedding, Lars called everything off. He needed to center himself, or something, and couldn't be married. I didn't know until later he was 'centering' himself with a yoga instructor named Jasmina. I was angry, and never gave him the ring back."

"Your engagement ring?"

"I sold it," she sniffed. "It cost a small fortune, and now the money has gone to a very good cause." She reached up and picked a piece of lint off Gavin's lapel. It was a little shared intimacy that wasn't lost on either of them. "Sorry," she croaked out when she realized what she was doing.

Clearing his throat, Gavin took half a step back, which was too bad. Ally missed his warmth.

"I like that you sold the ring and used the money for the town, but why buy a date?"

"Umm…yeah, that."

He stepped into her space again, knowing it affected her, and this time his scent, subtle and musky, surrounded her. God. She was a goner already. This was not a good idea. What the hell was she thinking?

"Ally? The date?" His voice, low and steady, wrapped

around her.

"I'm an event planner, and my firm planned a destination wedding for a close friend of mine." This was much harder than she imagined. Now that she actually had to ask him about going with her, she reconsidered. She was such a chicken. "Maybe this is a bad idea."

"You don't want to go to the wedding alone. Is that it?"

"Not really, but you know what? Forget it. We can go out to dinner or something. Catch up."

"Ally, that's an awfully expensive dinner."

"Maybe, but…" She took a deep breath. "This is awkward."

He laughed. "No, considering our history, you buying me for twenty-five grand is awkward—this is just you losing your nerve."

He was right about that. Ally had never been more terrified in her life. "I'm reconsidering. I don't want to put you in a bad position, Gavin. I know we didn't part on the best terms."

"That's the understatement of the decade. Why don't you want to go to the wedding alone? If it's a friend, you'll know people."

"Because my ex will be there. With his girlfriend."

"What was his name again?" Gavin chuckled sarcastically. "Odin? Olaf?"

Smacking his arm playfully, she had to smile, even though she wanted to cry. "Don't be an ass. His name is

Lars."

"Right. Lars."

"I don't want you to feel uncomfortable. This seemed like a good idea, until I saw the look in your eyes. I shouldn't have bid and just made a big donation instead."

"That would have left me with Jenny, and there was nothing good about that scenario."

"Really? This I gotta hear. I thought you two were buddies."

He scowled. "I'm not talking about it. But we are not 'buddies,' as you put it. And what do you mean the look in my eyes? How did I look at you?"

Ah, shit. She didn't want to get into this. There was no way for her to explain what was going on in her head without sounding whiny and pitiful. That girl had left the building a long time ago.

"You didn't look happy to see me." It was the truth. And it was understandable.

"I was surprised. It's been what? Almost ten years? And, uh… you look different. I mean I knew it was you, but, you look different. But other than the money being thrown around, I don't think I did anything."

"I've lost weight. I'm not fat anymore."

"You weren't fat to begin with."

"I was…"

He stopped her with a wave of his hand. "You were beautiful then, and you're beautiful now. It's just different.

That's all."

People were leaving the bar since the auction was over, and Gavin was very aware of everyone, waving goodnight as they walked past. He still lived here, whereas most people didn't even recognize her. She guessed he was pretty embarrassed by the attention.

"I'm so sorry, Gavin. I never even thought about how the bidding would affect you. How embarrassing it would be."

"I'm not embarrassed. You seem more affected than I am." He sat on a bench outside the bar. "Same old Ally. Worried about other people's opinions."

"Lovely. Thanks for that." Nothing like being insulted.

"Just stating a fact."

She wasn't the same girl who left Marietta High School. Awkward and shy, Ally was the band geek, an eternal romantic who wrote love stories to pass the time. She wasn't thin, or athletic. She never felt particularly pretty. And her insecurities did put her at the mercy of others. That girl was long gone, at least most of the time.

She'd worked hard to pack away all the baggage, and focus on being a success. She'd built a life for herself in Seattle, and fought past all the old insecurities while doing so. If she hadn't, she would have been a hot mess when Lars dumped her; instead, she pushed harder, worked harder, and made her own life even better.

But all that focus inward didn't leave a lot of time for relationships. When she finally came up for air, Ally realized she was pretty lonely.

Of course, the girl she used to be would make an appearance occasionally. The one who was scared or unsure, who doubted herself, or who doubted others? She was still in there. The doubter was the one who'd walked away from Gavin on the say so of an angry, desperate, mean girl, instead of having faith in her best friend—the boy she loved so much it hurt.

Their unlikely friendship developed in grade school. They'd bonded over their love of books, spending long afternoons in the library sharing stories and reading. But in high school, they got even closer. She loved her girlfriends, but Gavin was different. He understood her need to know things. To study. And even though she didn't play sports, he appreciated that she was competitive.

He was a golden boy. A star athlete, super student, from a large well-known family, his shyness was endearing. She sensed he still was. They spent a lot of time together, and Ally actually thought she might have a real love story for once.

Eventually, it all fell apart because she was an idiot.

Before he left for college, Gavin had made it clear that he wanted to be more than friends and that his feelings ran deep. He stayed in touch with her, religiously calling and texting. They saw each other over the holidays, but since Ally was traveling to family on the East Coast, they didn't have any real time together.

It was right after that that Jenny got inside her head, and Ally made the mistake of believing the worst about Gavin.

"I'm sorry," she whispered. "I'll understand if you don't want to do it."

"Let me think about it," he said, his voice more tender than she deserved.

"Fair enough." Ally couldn't ask for more than that. She extended her hand and he hesitated before grasping it firmly. Touching him was another mistake. Tingles ran right up her arm, circling around and settling in the vicinity of her heart. "Let me know. I'll leave my number with Rowan."

"Just put your number in my phone," he snarled. "I don't need Ro in on this."

Handing her his phone, she keyed in the number and hit save. He then texted her, so she had his.

"There," he said. "No Rowan."

"Okay. Let me know. The event is two weeks from Saturday, but I'm heading up the Thursday before and staying until Monday. It's at Whispering River Ranch."

"That luxury resort in the mountains? That's not one of those places where city folks go to play Wild West, is it?"

"Hardly, cowboy." Ally giggled. "It's all about relaxing. You can ride if you like, but it's not a working ranch anymore. I'm planning on several spa treatments."

"Spa treatments. Ooo-kay. I'll let you know in a couple of days. If I can't, I'm sure you can get your money—"

"No." She cut him off. "The money stays with the event.

I don't want it. At least that damn ring went for a good cause."

"Fine. I'll talk to you then. 'Night."

As quick as he appeared, he was gone. And once Gavin went into Grey's, Ally went back to the position she'd been in when he first walked outside. She leaned against a lamppost and curled forward. She felt like she was going to throw up.

GAVIN TUNED OUT the people calling his name, and shot right up the stairs, seeing Nick and Cassidy on the way down. There was a story there. Code and Hayley? Jesus. This night was turning into a fucking nightmare, just like Colt said it would. At that point, all Gavin knew was there wasn't a chance in hell he was going to talk to anyone until he could process what had happened. Of all the people to walk back in his life, Ally was the last one he expected to see.

And, man, had she changed.

Slender and sophisticated, she still possessed her razor sharp wit, but it was delivered with an indifference he'd never noticed in her before. Ally had always cared. About everything. She might have been a little shy, but it was that genuine sweetness that he liked the most about her. Now she was practical. Focused.

The dreamer was gone.

In her place was a successful, pragmatic businesswoman

with long, wavy cinnamon colored hair, deep brown eyes, and legs that went on forever. He'd seen gorgeous women before. Hell, they were bidding on him ten minutes ago. But there was always something special about Ally, a sexy vibe that drove him to distraction as a teenager. He thought it was gone, the attraction—but when he shook her hand, the jolt that went through him told him otherwise. She may have looked different, but his girl was still in there. Fancy clothes, perfect make-up, and a few pounds weren't going to change that.

Spending time with her was definitely playing with fire. And Gavin had no desire to be burned again.

"Holy shit, Clark." Gavin didn't know who said it because Code and Colt burst into the upstairs room at the same time and slapped him on the back.

"Twenty-five grand?" Code said. "That girl must be doing all right for herself if she can drop twenty-five-large on your sorry ass."

"Her fiancé dumped her last year. She sold the ring and used the money for the auction." The minute he said it, Gavin regretted giving up Ally's secret.

"Creative," Colt added. "And a nice burn to the asshole. Cheers to the little lady." He lifted his beer bottle in salute.

"Yeah. *Cheers.* She's an event planner," he volunteered. "Wants me to go to a destination wedding in a couple of weeks because the ex is going to be there."

"Wow. I guess she wants her money's worth," Code

chuckled.

"She won't hold me to it. If I don't want to go, won't press the issue, and will let the donation stand."

The guys went silent, meaning they were impressed, or they were trying to think of something funny to say. He hoped it was impressed, because they were rarely funny.

"What are you going to do?" The question, serious and not the least bit sarcastic, came from Colt.

"I'm thinking about it." *He didn't know how he was going to tell Ally he couldn't be alone with her for a long weekend.*

"She is *hot*. She wasn't that hot in high school," Colt muttered.

Gavin really had to keep his temper from flaring because punching one of his best friends wouldn't be a good way to end the night. But Colt wasn't wrong. Her geeky charm had gone to high level gorgeous, and she didn't even look like she was trying.

Coach D and his wife entered the room, misty eyed, stopping the conversation. "You boys made it happen. We are over our fifty-thousand-dollar goal. The hospital will get the helipad, possibly before next winter."

Mrs. Downey hugged all of them, giving Gavin a pat on the cheek for good measure. "I had no idea that was Allison Beaumont until she wrote her check. I remember how sweet you two were with each other. She's lovely, and so generous. I hope you have a wonderful time with her. Where are you going on your date?"

That was why he did this. He had the gratitude of one of the nicest women on Planet Earth, he'd helped his former coach, and hopefully the addition of the helipad would make sure no one would have to lose a child simply because of timing.

"A destination wedding in the mountains," he said. "She doesn't want to go dateless."

"That will be fun! And very romantic."

Romantic. Right. He was dead. "It will be nice to catch up, and I hear the ranch resort is pretty spectacular."

The entire Downey clan joined them, including Troy's mother, who knew Gavin from the night Troy died. She gave him a hug, and whispered her thanks, adding, "*For everything.*"

It was and emotional meeting, and it woke Gavin up to one thing. Any petty problem he had with Ally could be put aside. He'd help her out.

Once Coach and his wife left the room, Gavin took out his phone and opened a text.

It's Gavin. I'm in.

The response didn't take long to come back.

Really?

Yes, really. What an attitude she had. *Let's meet for lunch to discuss details.*

Okay. Diner tomorrow? Around noon?

Sure. See you then. Right in the middle of town, where there was no hiding from the nosy bodies. The gossip would be flying.

Just what he always wanted.

HE SAID YES. It could all go to hell, Ally knew that, but staring at her phone, she wondered what made him decide in her favor. She was standing at the bar, sipping celebratory champagne. Not only had the auction beaten the one the previous year, but the fundraising goal had been surpassed by thousands. Rowan raised her glass.

"To our glorious bidders. We wouldn't be making improvements to the hospital without your generous donations." Rowan gave her a big hug. "I never would have suspected you to throw down that kind of cash."

Ally nodded. That's because back in school, only a few people really knew her, Gavin being one of them. And thinking about it, even he was surprised. "I guess I've gotten bolder. But it was a good cause."

Vivi sidled up to her at the bar. "So where are you going on your date? Tell us."

Ally didn't want to be pushed, especially not until she'd had a chance to talk to Gavin tomorrow. "We haven't decided. I guess we'll know soon enough."

She wasn't going to be railroaded, and she wasn't about to gossip. Nope. If she knew anything about Marietta, it was that the walls had ears, and anything she said would get back to Gavin before she had a chance to feel him out.

Her heart was still pounding from their quick encounter.

The man was potent, serious, and not about to take any shit. There was a reason he said yes to the date, and she figured it had very little to do with her.

If he wasn't going to make it work, Ally was ready to tell him to forget it. She wanted a date, but she had no intention of being humiliated, nor did she want him miserable. This wedding was her firm's crowning glory, and she wanted people to have fun.

Hopefully, Dr. Clark would be on board. If not, she'd manage on her own, just like always.

Chapter Four

A LLY WANDERED INTO the kitchen of her family house and felt the warm fuzzies wash over her. Her parents, married thirty-five years, were holding hands at the breakfast table. They were chatting about something Dad was showing her mother on his tablet, and Mom was giggling and asking questions.

They were her example for a good marriage. It wasn't perfect. They'd had their ups and downs, but they never gave up on each other. No matter what.

"Oh! Ally! You're up. I made a breakfast pie, it's keeping warm for you. Do you want coffee?" Her mother fussed. She loved to fuss.

"Mom. I can make a cup of coffee. Sit."

Settling back in her chair, she knew the questions would come any second. They would give it some time, let air swirl around a bit before asking anything There was no doubt her parents had heard about her massive bid at the auction. But she had no idea if they knew anything else.

They weren't talking. Ally pressed the button on the brewer and waited for her coffee.

Still nothing.

She doctored the contents of the mug with a little sugar and a heavy dollop of cream.

Still nothing.

It was driving her nuts.

"So how was the auction?"

Finally! Her father opened the conversation. They wouldn't understand about the amount of money she dropped. Well, they might. Neither of them had liked Lars, so selling his ostentatious ring probably would have been fine with them. But the number was, as Gavin said, obscene.

"Anything unusual?" Mom pondered.

"Why are you asking when you already know?"

"Why do you think that?" Her father said innocently.

Something about being homemade Ally channel her inner teenager. She rolled her eyes. "Dad, this town is wired. Whether it's pure gossip, or some kind of cosmic woo woo, everyone knows everything."

Her parents exchanged one of *those* glances. She hated that.

Her mother grinned. "Your winning bid was *something*."

Ally shuffled her feet, as she sipped her coffee. More inner teenager.

"It's not a problem," her dad added. "It's just not really like you. It was very... forward."

"Forward. Right."

"Did you talk to Gavin?" Her mother always liked

47

Gavin, and even though Ally had tried to keep her feelings about him between her and her two close friends, her mom always knew. Which meant her dad knew.

"Yes. He was annoyed. And he says he wasn't, but I think he was embarrassed. I'm meeting him for lunch later to talk about the date."

"Why was he embarrassed? It was for a good cause. And he gets to spend time with you." She loved how her dad jumped to her defense.

"I'm guessing because it was me. And history, you know."

Not listening to a word that was said, her mother continued. "Do you have something in mind? For the date?" Mom was probably ready to suggest something. The woman was a fountain of ideas.

"I do. I'll let you know how it goes."

Her father rose from his chair and kissed her mother on the cheek. "I'll bring home something for dinner." He smiled at Ally. "Will you be joining us?"

"Sure thing, Dad."

Rob Beaumont, her father, was a sweet man. Loyal. Hardworking. Devoted to his family. He taught science at the middle school, and was the boys' hockey coach. Her mother, who had just retired from teaching, had taken a part time job in the children's room at the library. Apparently, today was a late day because she was having after school story time; so since her dad's season was over, he happily picked up the slack around the house.

They worked as a team. They always had. And as corny or nosy as her parents were, they loved each other and her fiercely.

"When are you seeing Gavin?" Mom asked.

"Lunch. At the diner."

"Oh, perfect. Pop in at the library so I can debrief you." Her mother winked, but it wasn't funny and Mom's face sobered. "You're nervous, Miss Ally. Aren't you?"

"Very. I put him in a bad spot. That wasn't my intention. He's angry."

Mom rose and kissed her forehead. "He won't stay angry. That's not in Gavin's nature."

"He's not the same guy he was back in high school. He's harder." Grabbing her coffee, she walked onto the screen porch, attempting to make sense of the man she met last night. The view from the back of the house was beautiful, and one of the things she enjoyed as much as possible when she came home.

Her parents' house was on the outskirts of town. Not far out, like some of the ranches, but they had about ten acres of pasture and a barn where they kept a few horses and a couple of small goats.

Orange Cat, who'd just shown up one day and took up residence in the yard with Fuzzy, their big gray calico, was stalking something by the western wall of the stable. Ally worried it was some poor little field mouse that had gotten into the feed room. It could also have been Fuzzy on the other side of the wall, teasing his partner in crime.

Dad had turned out all three horses before he left for work, and she could see them grazing by the hill stream. What struck her was the quiet. There was nothing like the peacefulness of morning on a farm. Watching her favorite gelding dash around the paddock, she had in her mind to take a ride later on.

Ally hadn't been on a horse since the last time she was home, over six months ago. She'd missed that, too. The time she spent grooming and riding were a natural mood elevator. Just being around the farm helped settled her mind. The more she thought about it, the more she wondered why she'd gone to live in a large city.

"Is he really that different?" Mom had joined her on the porch, taking up the position beside her.

Ally smiled. Her mother, who was a petite brunette, always called her taller daughter a Celtic warrior. The problem was Ally never felt like a warrior. Nah. She was much more wimp than warrior. Gavin made her even more unsure of herself. "He is different, something has affected him, changed him. But I still can see his compassion. He cares about people, you know? The way he hugged Mrs. D, and Coach. He really cares."

Her mother hesitated, then sat in one of the wicker chairs they kept on the porch. "Did you know Gavin was the attending physician in the Emergency Room when Troy was brought in?"

"What? No. I didn't." Ally couldn't imagine what Gavin had gone through. All the guys on the team loved that kid. Troy was like a little brother.

"He met the LifeFlight. Was there with Troy's mother when the boy was declared dead. Gavin did everything he could. The whole trauma team did. But it wasn't enough."

Ally's heart was breaking for Gavin. Knowing the kind of person he was, she could only imagine what he was going through. "My God. What a nightmare."

"I just thought a little perspective would help you."

Maybe not help, but she understood better, and that was a plus. It was possible that the wedding, and the time away, would be good for him. Ally considered that Gavin might need a little push, and she had every intention of giving it to him.

GAVIN ARRIVED AT the diner right around noon, and as soon as he walked in the door and the different food aromas hit him, he realized how much he was craving a burger with crispy fries. Scanning the room, he saw the back of Ally's curly red head in a booth at the far side of the restaurant.

He waved to Paige Joffe, the owner of the diner, and made his way to where Ally was sitting. She'd been on his mind since last night, including a dream that had them in a bed, hot, sweaty, and very naked. It was so real he could still feel her.

Not a great thing to have on his mind when he had to have lunch with the woman. If he was honest with himself, dread aside, he'd been looking forward to it. He was curious about the destination wedding she was planning, and put simply, he liked having her around again.

They'd had minimal contact after the auction, just a conversation, but for the first time in over a year, he felt a spark. Something snapped inside of him, and he thought about going on that date rather than holing up in his office with journals and medical texts on traumatic brain injuries.

As he got closer, he heard her voice; she was on the phone with someone, and there were binders and planners open all over the table. It looked like controlled chaos. Lapsing in and out of French, Ally was muttering something about the menu under her breath and he figured she was planning a wedding in France. Master of the obvious.

When she slammed the flat of her hand on the table and startled everyone in the place, Gavin realized this was crisis management, not chaos. "Gustav!" she shouted. "Écoute-moi! J'ai besoin de savoir si la pâtisserie peut faire un gâteau sans gluten." She breathed out. "*Non, non.* Of course I'm not joking. I know a gluten-free cake from a famous French bakery is somewhat *unusual.*" She paused, and Gavin could hear Gustav yelling at her. He couldn't discern the language, but it wasn't pleasant. "No?... The answer is no... Okay. Okay, fine...*Oui.* I've got it. No."

She pressed the screen on her phone, disconnecting her call, and tossed it on the table. "Dammit. I wish I knew how to say asshole in French."

She was muttering to herself, and Gavin found her really appealing at that moment. Angry and exasperated, she was ridiculously attractive. He slid into the bench facing her and smiled.

"That sounded intense."

"Hi. Yeah, it was. I'm so pissed—at the vendor *and* at the dopey bride and groom. You want to have an artisanal, organic, gluten-free, dairy-sensitive, fat-free, farm-raised pescatarian reception? Don't pick the food capital of the world as your location, and then insist on *one* particular bakery, run by an elderly French couple who think flour and butter rule the world, to make your wedding cake."

"I guess that wouldn't be the best idea. Where were you going to have your wedding?"

The question obviously shocked her, but he had to know the answer if they were going to fool her friends at the wedding in two weeks. If he was going in as her boyfriend, he had to know everything about her. Even about her breakup.

"Oh, uh… that was out of the blue."

Obviously painful, he found he wanted to punch the idiot who hurt her. Yeah, just like old times. "Yep. Give it up."

She let out a long breath. "We'd planned a beautiful reception on Orcas Island, in the northwest corner of

Washington. The location is one of the prettiest places I've ever seen."

"And he just decided he didn't want to be married?"

"I don't know about that. He decided he didn't want to marry me."

Ouch.

"He'd been cheating on me. I told you that."

"He's an idiot, then?"

Taking a sip of her coffee, she grinned. "I think I used more colorful language than that."

"I'm sure you did."

"Let me clean up this mess. I didn't expect to get stuck on a call." She started closing books and stuffing papers back into her briefcase. Based on what he saw, her business was complicated.

"Is it just you, or do you have employees?"

"I have two other event planners. One handles weddings and the other does different kinds of events, corporate gatherings, smaller intimate parties. I also have three administrative assistants and a lot of people who work on contract, so managing all that can get a little crazy."

"And you still plan weddings?"

"The bigger or more expensive ones, yes. Which is why I end up with these ridiculous requests."

"It's impressive. Do you like your work?"

"I do." She nodded, and he could see in her eyes she meant it. "It was hard after my own wedding was cancelled.

It made a little sidebar in one of the newspapers since Lars is a very big deal on the social circuit."

"What does he do?"

"Hedge fund manager. He makes the rich tech guys in Seattle even richer. The only reason he agreed to the smaller venue on Orcas was because it looked more exclusive. Otherwise the guest list would have topped three hundred."

That did not sound like her kind of guy. Ally was all about feelings and sentimentality. This guy sounded like a pretentious ass. "How did he end up with Yoga Girl?"

"He's gotten into the whole inner peace thing. I mean, I like to relax as much as anyone, but he said I threw off his aura or something. I'm too intense. I don't know. Apparently Jasmina centers him."

"Centers him?" The guy sounded like a complete nutcase. "Does he really practice the lifestyle or is this all for show?"

"What do you think?" she asked. Picking up a pen, she started flipping it between her fingers. "I deal with so much on my own. I'm not incompetent or helpless. I run a business that does very well, I bought my own place. I have investments. I have friends. But I don't want to face this by myself." She looked away, thinking, before looking him straight in the eyes. "I bid on you because I know you."

"I'm not the teenager you blew off, Ally."

"I know. But you're a good guy, Gavin." She shifted in her seat. "Lars always dumped on my small town upbringing.

He said he didn't know how I came out of Marietta with a shred of sophistication. I guess I thought someone from home, like you, could show him he's wrong."

In a strange way, he was flattered. On the other hand, she was looking for someone who fit the profile. "If I said I didn't want to go, you wouldn't push it?"

More than likely, he was going to go with her. But he wanted to see how she'd react to a possible no. That would tell him if they could make this work.

"Hmm. I was thinking about that, and I've decided I'm going to hold you to your agreement for a date."

He shouldn't have been surprised, but he was. This was a complete turn around from last night, and he was more than a little pissed off. "Are you serious?"

"Completely. *Your wish is my command...*" Ally folded her hands neatly in front of her after quoting what he 'offered' in the auction program. "Well, my wish is for you to accompany me to the wedding. It will be fun."

"For Christ's sake! I didn't write that, Rowan did. Take her to the wedding!" His voice boomed across the diner, causing heads to turn. Even Flo, the cook, poked her head out of the kitchen.

How had this happened? He'd have been better off making a big fat donation to the hospital fund rather than subject himself to this insanity. Between the four of them, he and his friends could have come up with the fifty thousand and none of them would have been going on these stupid dates.

"Are you done pouting, Gavin? Because I'd like to order lunch."

Ally opened her menu and leveled her gaze at him. He was so pissed off, but all he could see was her gorgeous face—her creamy skin, lush mouth and large round eyes which were surrounded by feathery dark lashes, clouded his brain.

But damn if she didn't push every fucking button. He was probably going to go with her, but he didn't like that she was forcing the issue. He was owed a piece of the decision making process considering their history.

Rising and sliding into her side of the booth, Gavin crowded her into the corner. She was no longer the heavier version of herself, but Ally possessed real-woman curves. Curves he'd dreamed about pressing into a mattress, and touching until she screamed his name.

"If you're going to push this, Ally, I want you to think about what it could mean."

"What are you doing?"

"Letting you know what you're up against." Running his fingers into the soft, spicy waves of her hair, Gavin cradled her head and kissed her.

Knowing the kiss was almost as big a mistake as the trip, Gavin wanted Ally to feel what they were up against. Five days alone at a romantic mountain ranch meant trouble. And neither of them could afford the trouble it would bring. He lived in Montana, she lived in Seattle. They were oil and water, and their history made them prime candidates for an emotional train wreck. The more he touched her, felt her, caught her scent, the more Gavin knew being alone with her was a bad, bad idea.

He had to show her because she didn't understand. Moving his mouth over her lips, creating the slightest bit of friction, Gavin sipped and teased until the first little sigh escaped on Ally's breath. Once her eyes drifted shut, she was all in.

That's when he knew they were both in trouble, because stopping didn't even occur to him. He continued to press his mouth to hers, pushing for more, and her response was to open her lips slightly until the tip of her tongue touched his. *Jesus.* Heat shot through him, making him hard immediately. Wanting her so much he hurt from it, Gavin pulled back.

Chapter Five

ALLY'S EYES FLUTTERED open and it took her a second to regain her senses. Gavin just stared into her perfect face. God, she was pretty. Her cheeks were flushed and her lips were puffy, swollen, from the kiss. Sucking in a sharp breath, he saw her lip start to tremble.

For a second he thought she was going to cry, and he was ready to apologize, but then from deep in her throat she hissed.

"Let me out of this booth."

"What?"

She shoved him. Hard. "MOVE. Let me out!"

"Ally, now do you understand? You and me together? I thought we could handle it, but we can't." He rose from the seat as she frantically gathered her things.

"Are you kidding me, Gavin?" She stood and when he reached out, she slapped his hand away. "Are you saying you kissed me to prove a point?"

"You're making a scene," he said firmly.

The flush started in her neck and rose through her face. Her eyes were blazing. Damn, she was furious. "I'm making a scene? I don't even know how to respond to such stupidity. YOU made the scene. You."

She turned and marched toward the door, her hair flying, and her steps long and fierce. Every person in the place was dead silent, shifting their gaze from her to him and then back. He'd never been so uncomfortable. This story was going to be told in town for years.

"Ally," he called out, pointing his finger at her for emphasis. "I'm right, and you know it."

He was so out of his league with her it wasn't even funny, but here he was, still trying to be *the guy*. To be right no matter what.

Asshole.

She spun towards him, and for a second he really thought she was going to let an f-bomb or two fly. But she maintained her composure, at least somewhat, and kept her response PG. "Go to hell, Gavin."

Not wasting another second, Ally stormed out of the diner, and he watched her head toward the library. When he stopped to look around, everyone was staring at him like he was an ax murderer. Shit. All he'd done was kiss a woman in public.

Granted, it was a great kiss, but it probably wasn't the kind of kiss some of the kids who were having lunch should have seen. There were tongues involved. Heavy breathing.

It was a really dirty kiss.

Okay, so he screwed up.

He was about to say something, but thought twice, and walked back to the table to retrieve his jacket. Paige the owner, gave him a death stare. There was no other way to describe it. She didn't say a word about what had just happened, just stared him down.

"Good day, Doctor," Paige said with an edge.

"Yeah," Gavin grumbled as he headed out. "That's debatable."

ALLY WENT STRAIGHT home. She didn't stop to see her mother, or walk around town like she planned. She didn't take advantage of the gorgeous spring day. She didn't eat at her favorite place.

It was all Gavin's fault, the dumbass. That kiss. What the hell was he thinking with that kiss? It was tender, deep, hot. So, so hot.

So, instead of all the things she was planning to do, she was at home, changing into her favorite pair of working jeans and boots, and on her way out to the barn. If she was going to be mad, she might as well work it off.

Grabbing a pitchfork and a wheelbarrow, she started cleaning the stalls, ridding each one it of old bedding and manure, scrubbing water buckets and refilling them, and stuffing hay bags.

After two hours detailing the stalls, she moved to the tack room, and that's where her father found her cleaning bridles and bits, probably one of the most thankless jobs in any barn.

When her dad came in and sat down next to her on the long bench, neither of them spoke. Ally had been fighting her emotions all afternoon, but her father didn't do anything except stick close. It was a routine they'd perfected when she was a geeky teen and nothing went right for her, including Gavin Clark.

"I should be smarter than this," she mumbled. "He got to me again, and I set myself up for it."

"How do you figure that? You went to a charity event. You didn't stalk the man." He wrapped his arm around her shoulders. "You're human. Don't be so hard on yourself."

"He was right about one thing; we shouldn't be around each other."

"He said that?" Her father was looking rather annoyed.

"I mean look at me. I'm a basket case. And nothing's ever going to change. He's not going to forgive me. We won't be friends again. What was I thinking?"

"I don't know about that. I think you're important to him, but boys, and some men, have a hard time getting where they need to be. You either have to wait it out, or do like you're planning and let it go. But friends? You two were *friends*, honey, but not really."

"We were friends! We were!"

"Sure. Maybe when you were ten." Her father was so matter-of-fact sometimes it was annoying. "What are you going to do?" he asked.

That was the big question. "I should forget about it, go to the wedding alone, and just be happy I helped the hospital."

"Well, sure. Avoidance is always safer, there's no risk."

Ally went back to scrubbing the bit she had in her hand. "That sounds good to me. Look where risking my heart has gotten me."

"I'm not following."

She blew out a breath, absently rubbing a rag over her favorite snaffle bit. "Lars was a risk. We were so different, but it seemed right. He was smart and exciting…"

"He's a self-absorbed moron, honey. Consider that bullet dodged."

"I guess. Then with Gavin, I don't know. I messed that one up. I know you don't think we were friends, but we were. Maybe I'm just not meant to be with anyone."

"Ally, get over yourself."

"Excuse me?"

"Go grab a horse and take a ride. Blow off some steam, but stop this 'poor me' stuff. You aren't the first person who's been burned in a relationship, or who's made a bad choice."

"Thanks for the sympathy, Dad."

"Honey, what do you want me to say? That Gavin shouldn't have kissed you like that? I'm your father, of course I'm going to say that. That Lars was a mistake? I thought so from the first time I met him."

"So? What's your point?"

"My point is: what do you intend to do about your date with Gavin? It's that simple. Lars, high school, it's all out of the picture."

Letting that sink in for a bit, she had to admit, she didn't know. Part of her wanted to drive out to his parents' ranch, drag him into the barn, and show him what a real kiss was like, among other things. The other part of her wanted to go straight back to Seattle and forget he ever existed.

She disagreed with her dad about one major point; their past did play a big role in the people they'd become. Ally was a better person because of her relationship with Gavin. She never doubted that.

More than likely, the right thing was somewhere in the middle, even if wild sex with Gavin, who was hotter than the surface of the sun, definitely had its appeal.

Playing with buckles and pulls, she reassembled the bridle and stood. "I need a shower."

Her father stood as well and gave her a comforting hug. It was the kind of hugs reserved for fathers. "What are you going to do?"

"I think after I'm clean, I'm going to head out the Clarks' ranch. I have a few things to say to Gavin."

Her father laughed. "I bet you do."

IT HAD BEEN twelve years since Ally had driven herself to the Clark Ranch. Settled generations ago, it sat in the foothills of the Absaroka range, southeast of Marietta. Their land was gorgeous—a combination of pasture, old growth trees, and streams teeming with fish, it was 600 acres of Montana perfection. It wasn't the biggest spread in the area, but it was ridiculously beautiful.

The clapboard house was built in the 1890s by Gavin's great-great-grandfather; it was large, with at least six bedrooms, a huge kitchen, and a front porch that wrapped around the whole house. Barns and stables dotted the landscape close by, and his mother's kitchen garden, with its just-tilled soil, was on the south side of the house. Ally remembered helping Mrs. Clark pick vegetables and herbs for dinner. When you were at the Clarks', everyone helped out.

Sitting in her car, Ally steeled her nerves. She'd worn something deliberately and overtly feminine and she had no idea why. It almost felt mean, but it was her only defense at this point, other than killing him, and she didn't want to go that far.

Her long, flounced skirt was gauzy and light, made up of several layers of brown fabric, and sported intricate embroidery and a tiny bit of ruffling. It was a gorgeous piece she bought from a local textile artist when she was driving through Oregon. She'd paired it with a soft, fitted pale pink Henley shirt and her best boots. There was a big belt, great jewelry, and she'd done her hair and makeup.

Her father claimed she was going to make Gavin cry. That was doubtful. Climbing out of her rented SUV, she pulled her wrap close around her shoulders as a stiff breeze blew through the valley. Ally figured if anything, he'd be annoyed, but after that kiss today, she agreed—he deserved to cry a little.

She had.

Climbing the short flight of stairs to the front door, Ally knocked purposefully. It was five-thirty, which meant it was quite possible she was interrupting dinner, something not generally recommended on a working ranch.

As usual, her timing was less than ideal.

She waited at the door, hearing people inside, but no one answered her knocks. As she started to make her way around to the kitchen door, she ran smack into Gavin, who was dirty, sweaty, and sexy as hell. He wasn't shirtless, but that didn't matter. His plain white t-shirt was stuck to his body showing off every defined muscle. Mother of God.

He grasped her arms and steadied her on her heels as she wobbled. "I thought I heard someone out here. Are you okay? I nearly bowled you over."

"Yeah, I'm fine. I'm…" Her breath shuddered being so close to him. The scent, the sweat, the defined muscles sent her hormones on a one-way trip south. One touch, and everything inside of her burned. "I came over to talk to you. But if it's a bad time, I understand."

"I went out and fixed about a mile of fence," he said with a smirk. "I needed to blow off some steam."

Ally knew that feeling all too well. "The stalls at home are pristine. I even scrubbed walls and water buckets."

"Ah. Yeah. Sounds like we had the same idea. So what brings you out here? You just want to yell at me and get it over with?" He wiped his face with a plaid flannel shirt he was holding, and Ally didn't know how long she was going to be able to hang on before she jumped him. The man was that irresistible.

"Yell at you?" She shook her head. "No. Like I said, I wanted to talk to you."

"Okay. You look really pretty, by the way. Beautiful."

Ally gave herself a quick look, happy that he noticed, but nervous because of the way he made her feel. He wasn't supposed to do this to her anymore. She wasn't supposed to be affected by him. "Thank you."

"What do you want to talk about, Ally?" He leaned against the porch rail, looking casual, confident.

Sexy.

Really, really sexy.

Crap.

"About the weekend. I know you don't want to go, so…"

"It's not that I don't want to. It sounds awesome, actually. And if things were different between us, it would be a great time. But can't you see how hard it would be? For both of us." He hesitated, turning his back to her before finishing. "I mean, there's a lot of chemistry between us, but no common ground. Other than the fact that we knew each other once upon a time, what else is there?"

BOOM. With those words, Gavin dropped a truth bomb that blew up her insides.

There was no way for Ally to know how much that statement would cut to the bone. But it did. It hurt. It hurt like nothing she'd felt in a very long time. Keeping his back to her, Ally was sure he didn't like being so blunt; he'd always been kind, and because of that, she felt the arrow go right to her heart.

Her lip started to tremble, her eyes burned. Oh no. She couldn't cry. No.

"I have to go." She couldn't get away from him fast enough. Bolting across the porch and down the steps, she heard Gavin's footfalls behind her. "I'll tell the organizers we went on a ride or something so you don't have to..."

She was almost to her car when he caught up to her.

"Ally, wait!" He grabbed her arm and spun her around.

Tears leaked from her eyes, tracking down her cheeks, and Gavin's expression softened immediately. Emotional manipulation was not her style, which was why she wanted to get away.

"Ah, shit. I didn't mean to make you cry."

"I know. I'm sorry. I don't cry a lot, but I guess... it's just... hearing you say that... Ugh. I hate this." Breaking away from him, she started yanking on the car door handle, but nothing was happening. "Shit. Why won't this open?" Turning her gently, Gavin wrapped her in his arms. As soon as she was pulled into his warmth, pressed against his strong body, the tears came harder and faster. This wasn't about romance. It wasn't about sex.

This was about her very best friend whom she'd hurt.

And she'd missed him. She'd missed him so much.

GAVIN HELD ALLY so close he could feel her heart beating. He dealt with life and death every day, but a crying woman brought him to his knees every damn time. That it was Ally grabbing onto his T-shirt made it worse. He held her head against his chest, whispered into her hair, anything he could think of to comfort her. And with each passing moment, he fell more and more under her spell.

Gavin had always been protective of Ally, ever since they were kids and she was picked on during recess. He beat up more than a couple of bullies for her, and took a lot of crap for it from the principal and his parents. But he wasn't going to let anyone make her unhappy.

By high school, he was done for. He adored her, but he was a hotshot football player and she was a band geek. Marietta was a great place, but the social hierarchy was alive and well in their high school. Neither one of them had enough nerve to cross the line from friendship to something more. But the summer before he left for college, things started to change.

At least, he'd thought they did.

"Come on. Let's talk." Brushing her tears away with his thumbs, he could see the hesitancy in her eyes. "Trust me, okay?"

She nodded and he felt awful, like he was the bully this time.

Grasping her hand, he led her to the enclosed gazebo near one of the barns. It was a large space they used for parties and events on the farm. It was outfitted with tables and chairs and some lawn furniture, including an old couch. Walking around the space when he closed the door behind them, Ally seemed to relax, even smiling cautiously.

"I remember the football parties you used to have here."

"Fun times. We drove my parents crazy, but they were glad we were all here instead of getting ourselves in trouble someplace else."

"I was so shy. I think I stood in the corner most of the time. You always wanted me there, but I felt strange. I don't think your friends liked me very much."

"That's not true. They liked you fine. But they didn't know you like I did."

That was true. "Fair enough."

Gavin walked to her and remembered that awkward girl with the wide smile who could beat him at his favorite video game, who loved movies, and books, and horses. He looked up and saw the dangling twinkle lights his dad kept strung in the rafters at the gazebo's peak. "I think this is where we had that dance the night before I left for college."

Her eyes went soft, almost pleading with him to let go of the memory. Tears threatened again as he pulled Ally into his arms.

"What was the song that was playing?" He knew. He'd never forget it, but he wanted to see if she did.

"*When You Kiss Me*," she whispered. "Why are we doing this? Are you still trying to make a point?"

Was he? Maybe. "I don't think so. When you're close, I go a little crazy. I'm sorry about today in the diner. I was out of line."

"You aren't the only one who goes crazy."

"We're probably going to regret it, but I'll go with you to the wedding. I can't get there until Friday though. Is that okay?"

"That's actually fine. It will give me a day to deal with all the logistics up front. I'll still have some work to do, but at least we'll be able to have some fun."

"We should probably set some ground rules," he said. "So we both understand the boundaries."

By this time, they were holding each other close and swaying to the music in their memories.

"Will the boundaries include dancing?" she asked as she looked in his eyes. "I mean, it is a wedding."

"Agreed. That wouldn't be a problem." It absolutely

would be. "But kissing would cross the line."

Ally nodded her agreement. "Sex is absolutely out."

Gavin froze. He didn't even realize she thought about sex with him. He, on the other hand, had been dreaming of making love to her since forever. "Of course."

They were still swaying to the imaginary music. "It kind of sucks that we'll miss out on that." Ally pulled back and leveled her eyes right at his, locking him in her molten gaze.

"The kissing?"

She grinned. "No, silly. The sex." Immediately, it was like someone flipped a switch. Ally froze in his arms. "*Damn.* I can't believe I said that out loud."

"Yeah." Gavin stepped back. "Me either."

"I'm so sorry," she said. "Of course, we'll have a room with a pull out sofa, or a second room, you won't have to worry about me losing my mind. I hope."

There would be nothing he'd love to see more than Ally cutting loose in bed. Just the way she made the comment about sex threw him into a meltdown.

"Sweet Jesus," she whispered. "I need to leave. It was the dancing. It made me... crazy." He watched her face flush from embarrassment. Gorgeous. "I... I haven't been touched like that in so long. It was nice."

There would be no hardship in touching her. He'd do it as much as she wanted, but at the same time, he was fighting to keep his physical response to her under control. Taking her in, everything about Ally was perfect, from her gorgeous hair and soft skin, to her big round eyes and her luscious curves... all Gavin wanted to do was put his hands on her. He was doing okay, until he caught her chewing on her plump, pink lips. That's when he snapped.

There was a catch in her breath when he pulled her into him, hard and tight, and lifted her up. Ally was right with him, though, arms looping around his neck and long legs slipping over his ass. Her skirt was riding up, showing the creamy skin of her thighs, and he had every intention of helping that skirt ride up a little more. His hands slid up, caressing the soft skin, and finally cupping the globes of her ass. Touching her was heaven, and with the slightest suggestion, he'd take her right there.

There were a couple of things wrong with his plan. First, the only place he could lay her back was an old picnic table. No. When he made love to Ally, he wanted her in a big soft bed that they'd stay in for days. Second, even though the gazebo was a distance from the house, it was too public for what he wanted to do to her.

"God—" Gavin was holding her so close, he could feel every muscle, every movement, every breath. His memory flashed back to nights she'd fall asleep on the couch, curled next to him, while they watched TV. He loved the way she felt, how she smelled. Even now, the light scent of baby shampoo tickled his nose.

"Gavin? Are you going to kiss me, or what?" Her breathing was heavy; he could see her pulse firing rapidly in her neck. She was as worked up as he was.

"Yeah," he replied. "Yeah."

And he did. They clung to each other while Gavin's mouth came down on hers with an edge of brutality. It was a consuming kiss, something meant to possess and devour. Earlier, when he kissed her in the diner, he'd been gentler, more deliberate, but this kiss was about control for him and for her. Their lips never stopped moving, allowing the friction to build; his tongue slipped into her mouth and she welcomed him, teasing it with her own.

This was the kiss they were too scared to share in high school, that they shouldn't be sharing now because their paths were too different. But this woman, who pressed herself against his erection, who nibbled his neck and who made the most wonderful dirty noises, deserved all of him.

Gavin moved his hands from her ass to her hips; gripping her, he let his thumbs travel underneath the wispy edge of her panties. He teased the soft folds, and as she ground into his hand, welcoming the intimacy, Gavin felt warm wetness. She was ready for him, if that's where they wanted to go.

Arching slightly, Ally tossed her head back, as little sounds escaped her throat. She smiled. "God, that feels so good. Going away together is probably a really bad idea."

"Or a really good one," he ground out. "Damn, Ally." Her perfume—light and floral, feminine—gave him a buzz. Resting his head on hers, he let it seep into him. "You feel so good. Smell so good."

WEEKEND WITH HER BACHELOR

Her head dropped onto his chest, and she made another little sound in her throat. "And you smell so... *bad*."

Stepping down and back, Ally squinted her eyes at him. "Holy hell, Gavin," she said on a laugh. "I know you were working on the fences, but did you roll in horse shit, too?"

Dumbfounded, it took him a second to catch what she said. He smelled *bad*? Sniffing his own armpits, he reeled. Then, he laughed, because the reaction was so Ally. Honest, no bullshit, she could always tell him the truth. The mood was broken, but that was probably a good thing.

That moment, strange as it was, drove home how much he'd missed her. But knowing they had to move past their near sex experience, he dished an insult right back.

"Excuse me, *Princess*," he snapped sarcastically. "I didn't just clean a few stalls today. I really worked."

She stuck her tongue out at him in defiance, and the two of them dissolved into fits of laughter. It felt good to laugh like this, to sit with someone who knew you well, and find the humor in an awkward situation. Thank God she'd stopped where they were headed. Gavin was two seconds from carrying her behind the big barn and making love to her against the wall. They might not have even got that far.

Even if it were the greatest sex of his life, the fallout would have sucked for both of them.

"I think we dodged the bullet there." Ally sat on a picnic bench and crossed her legs. "That would have been awkward."

"The sex would have been amazing." Beyond amazing, more than likely. Gavin already missed the feel of her. "But yeah, you're right."

"Amazing, but awkward," she agreed.

He sat next to her and patted her knee. "Nice save."

Her face softened and she dropped her head to the top of his shoulder. It was how they'd always been with each other. Close. Affectionate. It was nice. "You're a fantastic kisser," she said.

"You're pretty good yourself."

"Pretty good?" She was mildly indignant at his assessment.

"Gavin! Ally! I know you two are in that gazebo." His eyebrows shot up as he heard his mother call from the house. "Come in to supper or I'll send your brothers out to embarrass the two of you."

"Great. We'd better get inside." He grabbed her hand, and the moment wasn't lost on either of them. Touching her was as natural as breathing to Gavin. He just didn't think they had a chance.

"I think I'll go home."

"Mom won't accept that, and you know it. Once she knows you're here, you'd better be prepared to eat."

As if on cue, his mother called out, "I made smothered chicken, Ally! I know it's your favorite, so don't you dare go sneaking off."

Gavin bent over laughing when Ally's eyes went wide in

shock. "Did she hear me or something? That was weird."

"Nah, it's just Christine." Gavin loved his mother with all his heart, but how she knew some of the things she knew, freaked him out. "Come on. Let's eat."

Chapter Six

ALLY COULD HAVE flown back to Seattle for a few days to deal with some projects, but she decided to stick around Marietta for a while and work remotely. Hell, she was the boss and that's why she had a laptop and a cell phone. Gavin had left for Bozeman the day after their bone-melting kiss in the gazebo, but he wasn't really gone.

For the last few days, she'd been getting pretty regular text messages from him about their weekend, mostly concerning what he should bring with him. She'd sent him a list of clothes and gear, and since he was bringing his truck, he'd have plenty of room. She'd arranged for them to have one of the glamping tents. Part cabin, part tent, it was a more rustic approach to the lodge, while still having a lot of perks.

One of those perks was a pull-out sofa. There would be no need for them to share the king sized bed, and the more Ally thought about it, the better it was. Maybe they could be friends again. They'd gone on for years that way until their emotions started messing them up.

Lisa had suggested a friends-with-benefits arrangement with Gavin, but Ally didn't see how that would work. She and Gavin had a lot of strong feelings towards each other, and friends with bennies sounded like a disaster waiting to happen.

But her insides warmed at the thought of him touching her again. Memories from the other day, when he kissed her like a starving man and teased her close to orgasm, lingered in her mind. If she closed her eyes, she could feel him again.

The days she'd been home had been pretty perfect, even the tough ones. Ally found herself torn between her life in Seattle and the one she missed in Montana. For the first time in years, she had no burning desire to head back to the city she'd made her home, and she wished she knew why.

Being with her parents was nice, but it wasn't like she wanted to move back in. She loved town, but she could see it getting boring. There was no nightlife. Few restaurants. Trendy shopping was a big no. Yet the charm of it all had gotten to her.

Gavin had gotten to her, as well. And as long as she was in the same state, she felt more at peace.

Crossing Court Street, Ally made her way to the library. She was going to try lunch at the diner again. Hopefully with her mother she'd be able to actually eat a meal. People in town were still chattering about the soul kiss Gavin laid on her in public last week. It had caused quite the stir, and Ally was getting the side eye from more than a few women.

And for some reason, Ally didn't mind. She kinda liked it.

Being linked to Gavin romantically was strange for her, but again, she didn't care. Maybe it was because they weren't romantic, or maybe because it was keeping people guessing.

Also a new feeling for a girl who was known as being more than a little nerdy and predictable.

The library in Marietta was a small, pretty building that served the residents with a variety of programs. Her mother was thrilled to find a part time job working in the children's department when she retired from teaching elementary school.

Louise Jenkins, the children's librarian, was reading a story to a group of preschoolers and her mother was helping a young patron with a book on dinosaurs. It was a warm and wonderful place, and Ally smiled just taking in the vibe.

"Hey!" her mom cried out. "You're here."

"Shhhh," Ally chided. "It's a library."

"Let me get my purse and we can go. I'm starved!"

Ally walked around the children's room, looking at some old favorite books and browsing through some new books she'd never seen. Coming to the library was always special. From the time she was very little, to the study sessions with friends, the library had been at the center of her existence.

Her mother emerged and the two of them walked back across Court Street. Marietta was so predictable. The shops were practical, the food was good and simple, and the people were friendly and hardworking. Every place should be this way.

"So," Mom began once they were seated in a booth. "How go the plans for the big wedding?"

"Good," she answered. "Everything is confirmed. The ranch is ready for us. I think my dress will still fit after eating like a pig for the past week. The bride and groom are all set. I think it's going to go off without a hitch."

"That's lovely, honey. Have you heard from Gavin?" And there was the question she was waiting for. Her mother was downright giddy Gavin had agreed to go with her. She didn't say why, but she was ridiculously excited.

"I heard from him yesterday. He's fine. Busy, I guess." *That's it, Ally, keep it vague.*

"Is he looking forward to seeing you?"

"I guess you'd have to ask him, Mom."

They ordered their food and settled into small talk about the library, Mom's retirement, and her father who was on a new kick at home. He was trying to automate everything, from lights to music to when the heat went on. It was keeping him occupied, but it was driving her crazy.

It was a pleasant lunch. Ally was enjoying her loaded burger and fries way too much when her mother sent her into shock.

"Maybe you and Gavin could just be friends with benefits."

The rapid intake of breath when Ally heard her mother's statement forced her iced tea down the wrong pipe, and sent Ally into a choking fit. Gasping and coughing wildly, her mother came around to the other side of the booth and slid in, frantically trying to help.

Friends with benefits? Holy shit.

"Oh, oh! Raise your arms honey. Here, let me help!" The next thing she knew her mother was grabbing her wrists, pulling them up over her head. God, this was humiliating. "Goodness," her mother exclaimed. "You're a big girl!"

The entire diner was watching her coughing fit while her mother treated her like a three-year-old, holding her arms above her head, shaking them around, and patting her back. "Breathe, Ally. Atta girl."

"MOM! Stop!" The words came out on a hoarse growl as she tried to catch her breath. "I'm fine. Just stop."

All the eyes? Still on them.

"What was that all about?" her mother asked. "It wasn't the friends with benefits thing, was it?"

"Mom, please stop talking about it." Ally hoped if she kept her voice down, her mother would temper what she always called her 'teacher voice'.

"I don't see the problem. It's the perfect solution because face it, my dear, you seriously need sex." No such luck on the volume. Her mother rose and went back to her side of the booth, completely unaware that her voice had carried through the diner and had stopped everyone mid-bite. Again.

Ally was becoming quite the lunchtime attraction. *Great.* This would be all over town before supper.

Gavin would hear about it, too.

Craptastic.

"I'm available!" came a hopeful voice from the end of the diner.

The place erupted in laughter and Ally felt the heat rise in her face. Forget charm, this was the hell of small towns.

GAVIN SPRAWLED ON his couch, exhausted from another marathon shift. The last thing he wanted was visitors, but someone was banging on the door of his apartment. When he opened it, he found his brother Dan, carrying a six pack.

"What the hell are you doing here?"

Dan grinned as he made his way inside, tossing his hat on one of the chairs. "Hey to you too, bro."

"Something wrong?"

Choosing a space on the couch, his brother sat and plopped his booted feet on the coffee table, popped the top off a bottle of beer, and handed it to his brother. "I guess that depends on your point of view."

Gavin took a long pull from the bottle and sat next to his brother. A true cowboy, with ranching in his blood, Dan was probably the smartest of the five of them, but he had the least amount of formal education. A philosopher, a deep thinker, he only ever cared about working with the horses and had become known as one of the best breeders and trainers in the west.

Gavin was a doctor, Eli a lawyer, but Dan had a way of

seeing to the heart of a matter, which made Gavin wonder what had happened that he took the drive to Bozeman.

"Why don't you explain this to me instead of talking in code."

Dan rubbed his hand across his cheek. "Ally."

It seemed that was everyone's favorite conversation to have with him. Too bad he didn't want to talk about it. Gavin hadn't been able to get Ally out of his head since the kiss they shared in the gazebo. It gave him the kind of rush that said he and Ally would either be really good together or would be really bad for each other. This middle ground they were on at the moment wasn't going to last.

"What about her?"

"She was at the diner today having lunch with her ma, I don't know how it came up, but your name got tossed around with the term 'friends with benefits' attached. Ally was even more embarrassed when her mom said something, loud enough for everyone to hear, about Ally needing sex."

"For Christ's sake. Parents. They do it to us every time."

"Based on reports out of the diner, Ally just about crawled under the table when a few volunteers offered to help her out." Dan was chuckling and having a good time at Ally's expense, or Gavin's, depending on how you looked at it.

The thought of anyone making offers to Ally made Gavin's blood boil. Which was another problem. He was starting to feel things for her again. It was more than physical; he wanted her. All to himself.

They'd been texting, and there had been a few late night phone conversations that gave him a look at the woman she'd become. It was true she was no longer the girl he knew in high school. She was better. Yeah, she still had a huge heart, and was whip smart, but Ally was also accomplished, sassy, and five-alarm sexy. Pretty damn perfect.

He was screwed.

"She walks back into my life and everything gets complicated."

Dan laughed. "I remember watching you when the pair of you were in high school, and all I could think was that you two were going to love each other forever, or kill each other."

"She must have been so embarrassed."

Dan nodded. "I'm guessin'. What are you going to do? You have to go to that wedding with her in a few days. Are you rooming together, because that could prove to be a problem." Dan took a sip off his beer. "Or not, depending on your point of view."

"Fucking point of view. Of course it would be bad. She lives in Seattle. I live here. That doesn't make for an easy relationship. What am I supposed to do?"

Ally said they wouldn't have to worry about sharing a bed, but just being in the same room with her meant he'd be in a constant state of agony. The woman had him tied in knots.

Dan was no help, shrugging it off and grabbing for the remote.

"Comfortable?" Gavin asked.

"Yep. Good thing too, since I'm sleeping here."

"You are?" Gavin enjoyed the closeness he had with his family—most of the time. This was not one of those times.

"I'm drinking, it's late—I'm not going back to Marietta tonight. I'll be out of your hair early. Probably leave about five."

Perfect. Tomorrow he didn't have to be up at the butt-crack of dawn, and Dan was not his quiet brother. "I guess I'll go to the gym in the morning."

"If you'd get your ass back to the ranch more and do physical work, you wouldn't need a gym."

"I'll tell that to the crazed patient I wrestled to the floor this morning."

"Stubborn stallion kicked and tried to bite me today."

"Yeah, me too." Gavin stood and grabbed a book he'd been reading.

"What? Are you shittin' me?"

"Nope. Wouldn't think of it." He looked back at his brother, who'd flipped on ESPN. "Are we done with the pissing contest?"

Nodding, his brother asked another question. "Where are you going with Ally? Some ranch resort or whatever the hell it is."

Gavin sat on the arm of the sofa. "It's called Whispering

River Ranch. Hundreds of acres. It looks nice."

His brother took out his phone, and after a little searching came up with the destination. "Damn, this place is more than nice. Even the tents have big bathrooms."

"Yeah. I think we're staying in one of those big tents. She said they have sofa beds so we won't have to... ah... share."

"Well that's a damn shame."

"What are you driving at, Danny? I'm too fucking tired to play your mind games."

"Look..." Dan stood, walking to the window at the front of the apartment. He looked out, all while exacting a posture only a real cowboy could pull off. "You and Ally have been headed down this road for a long time. The two of you should be together. Why you're fighting it, I don't know, but the woman is smart, funny, and gorgeous. What's going on?"

"I don't know." Gavin ran his fingers through his hair. "Maybe I don't want to mess up a good thing." That was a lie. What they had going on wasn't good. It was torture.

"Right. You're scared."

"Scared? No."

"Sure you are, and you should be."

"Really. And you have all this relationship experience? I don't think you've had a steady girlfriend since you were in seventh grade."

Dan leaned back with a shit-eatin' grin on his face. "Yeah. Pam Belton. She let me kiss her after the Valentine's

Dance. Told me I got lucky."

"I guess when you're twelve…" Gavin chuckled, wishing things were that simple. Silence settled between them, awkward and telling. "Women."

"She's got you hogtied already, doesn't she?"

"You have no idea. I don't get affected like this. Not since I was in my teens."

"You mean since the last time Ally was around?"

Yeah, that's exactly what he meant, but he wasn't going into it any further. "Help yourself to whatever's in the kitchen. I'll see you before you leave."

LATER, STRETCHED OUT on his bed, Gavin picked up his phone and sent a text to Ally.

See you in a couple of days.

The response was almost instant. *Looking forward to it. Let me know when you're on your way.*

How are you holding up after today? His thumb hovered over the screen. He really hesitated before finally pressing send.

Not so instant this time. He waited. And waited. When she didn't answer, he figured he'd pissed her off, or embarrassed her. Or both.

Then his phone buzzed in his hand.

Ally. She was calling.

"Hey."

"Hi," she said, her voice barely there. "It's not too late, is it?"

"No. Are you alright?"

"How did you hear? I mean, I figured you would, but…"

In his mind, Gavin tried to picture what happened in the diner. Unfortunately, he kept seeing Ally's blissful expression after their kiss the week before. "My brother is here. He filled me in."

"Great."

"Don't let it get to you. There'll be something new for everyone to latch onto in a couple of days." It was true, but Gavin knew no one would ever forget it. The story would be around for ages.

"It was humiliating. It was bad enough it was so public, but that my mother thinks that I'm, I don't know, hard up, is the worst."

"I'm sure she doesn't think that."

"Yeah, she does. I know her heart is in the right place, but oh, my God. The place went into shock when she said '*you need sex.*'"

He laughed, even though he was trying hard not to. "Was the shock more, less, or equal to when I kissed you?"

He thought he heard a little sigh from her end, and that made him stupidly happy. Shit. He really hated when his brother was right.

"I don't know. Probably about equal. With you it was *show*, with Mom it was *tell*."

"Getting away won't be a bad thing, I guess."

"No. And then I'm going home, so…"

Right. Seattle was home. That was a huge difference between them. No matter where he was, Marietta was always home. That wasn't Ally's reality. "I'll see you in a few days. Let me know when you arrive at the ranch Thursday, okay?"

"Oh, yeah. Okay," she replied.

"Good." He was at a loss for what to say. His male brain failing him. "Hey, what are you doing tomorrow?" Damn. Why did he ask that?

"Nothing much. I was going to make some phone calls, hang out with my four-legged friends. Pack."

"I'm working, but not until ten at night. You want to drive up and meet some new four-legged friends?"

"Um. What do you have in mind?" She wasn't going to say yes. The drive was long, and she was going to see him in a couple of days, but he was in it now, so he had to explain.

"I have a friend from college who lives out here. He's a large animal vet. He has a stable full of horses and I go out to his place once a week or so and ride the trails."

"Oh, well—"

"I know it's a long drive, but I thought it could be a good distraction. Something to do. We can get our story straight."

She was quiet for a minute, and Gavin wondered what the hell he'd just stepped in.

"That sounds like fun," she said. "What time should I be there?"

"Um, is the morning okay? I'll take you for lunch after, and then I can get some sleep before heading to work."

"Text me the address and I'll plan to be there by ten?" She actually sounded like she was looking forward to it.

"Sounds good." He had a lot of planning to do. "I'll see you then."

"Good night, Gavin."

"Night, Ally."

The call ended and Gavin had to face one truth. Seeing her again had changed him. He'd been content being on his own, but now, she was in his head all the damn time. Thoughts of her consumed him. His brother was right about one thing; he was fucking scared of everything Ally represented.

Maybe it was time for him to get over it.

THANKFULLY, THE RANCH Gavin told her about wasn't hard to find. Ally didn't travel to Bozeman too often, generally making trips with her parents if they had business in the city. When she pulled in the parking area after traveling down a long, dirt driveway, Gavin was already waiting for her.

She knew he had a medical degree. But leaning hip shot into his truck, he was all cowboy. From his scuffed up boots, to his Wrangler jeans, to the well-worn hat on his head, this was a country boy through and through.

Ally had really missed country boys.

As her truck pulled in next to his, he was right there to open the door—and, surprisingly, pull her into his arms.

"Hey there, beautiful." He kissed her gently on the cheek. "How was your ride?"

"Fine, no traffic, the weather's great. I couldn't have asked for an easier trip." Ally grabbed a pair of boots from the backseat. "Tell me about the horses."

Gavin smiled. Why-oh-why did he have to do that? Then he took her hand, lacing his fingers through hers, he made her blush, made her ache. What was the man up to? This weekend could go in so many directions. All Ally hoped was that they would have a good time together. That they could leave the baggage behind, and even if they couldn't be lovers, maybe, just maybe, they could be friends again.

But what if there was more? What if they slept together? What if they found a way to be together? What would she do then? There were so many questions running through Ally's head, she often found herself going around in circles. She'd talked to Lisa about it, and her friend was of the opinion that Ally was thinking too much, and that she should just see what happened.

The problem was Ally was a planner. That was the reason she got into the business she did. She liked planning. She liked knowing how things were going to go. She liked order over chaos.

But no matter how hard she tried, it seemed whenever her heart got involved, chaos took over.

"This here is Pete." Gavin stroked the nose of a good size bay horse. A rich brown with a black mane and tail, he had kind eyes, and what looked to be a good sturdy back. He was already tacked up, and waiting for her.

Patting the horse's neck, Ally could feel the animal's gentleness. He was a good boy. "Hey, Pete. You ready to take a ride?"

Offering his hands, Gavin gave Ally a leg up into the saddle. Once she'd settled herself, and adjusted her stirrups and reins, she leaned over and gave Pete, who hadn't moved an inch, a pat and a hug.

Gavin trotted up beside her on a large, liver-colored chestnut, who answered to the name of Rio. "So, you want to give these two boys a workout?"

Ally wanted to give Gavin a workout. No doubt about that. Placing her straw Stetson square on her head, Ally grinned. "This is your neighborhood, show me around, Doc."

"All right then. Let's get on with this."

GAVIN HAD FORGOTTEN how deft Ally was on the back of a horse. For all the times she claimed she wasn't athletic, he would then see her climb on the back of a difficult mount and proceed to race barrels or jump fences. It didn't matter what it was; if Ally had a horse underneath her, she could do it all. Today was no different. They'd gone into the foothills of the mountains, with rocky trails and endless turns, and enjoyed watching her have such a good time. He was glad he'd asked her to come up.

They came to a clearing, a true grassy meadow with wild flowers blooming, and dismounted. He watched Ally stand completely still and look out at the acres and acres in front of her. She took a deep breath, like she was trying to remember, absorbing all the feelings that she only got when she was home. Gavin still had a hard time seeing Ally in the city. He had a hard time seeing her with a guy like Lars. He had a hard time thinking about her anywhere but here. With him.

Each of them held the horses' reins and their free hands reached for each other.

He was unbelievably screwed, unless he could find a way to make her want to stay.

Fortunately, Gavin had thought ahead enough that he brought a blanket to spread out on the grass. Once he did, Ally twisted herself down into a sitting position and then lay back, gazing at the ever-changing sky. "Do you ever look up? I mean, look at all the formations. There are so many things we don't know about yet. In some ways, the clouds we see are mysteries."

"You think way too much this early in the morning." But he looked up too. "I'm still on my first cup of coffee."

"Seriously?" she asked. "How can you be in such a high-stress, sleep-deprived, profession and not be mainlining caffeine?"

"I dunno. Maybe I don't want to die of a heart attack."

"Pssht. Details, details."

Leaning back, and propping himself up on his elbows, he took her all in. He wondered if she would bolt if he kissed her, if she knew how much he wanted to make love to her. "Any last-minute details to tell me about the wedding?"

"No, I don't think so. The team at the resort has been great; they keep me posted with everything they're doing. I almost feel redundant."

"Don't let your client hear that."

Turning on her side and facing him, Ally reached out and stroked a lock of hair from his face. Gavin wondered what was going through her mind. Was it just an absent gesture, something friendly, or something more intimate? He couldn't tell.

"Have you recovered from yesterday?"

Seeing how she cringed, almost gritting her teeth, Gavin hated that Ally was still suffering from the aftershocks. "I love my mother. But I didn't love her so much yesterday."

"I can imagine. If you don't mind my saying so, she really missed the mark."

"What do you mean? Missed the mark?"

"With you." Gavin lowered himself so he was flat on his back, and pulled Ally toward him, tucking her safely into the crook of his arm. "I just think there are times, there always have been, that your mama didn't really get you. She's a sweet woman, but I think you've always baffled her some.

For all your modern sensibilities, you are not a 'friends with benefits' girl."

"How do you know that?"

Kissing her forehead softly, Gavin pulled her closer. "I'm not saying you don't know your own mind, or that you can't make decisions for yourself, but you wouldn't make *that* decision."

"You don't think I do casual sex?"

"I know you don't."

Wiggling her way on top of him, Ally was nose-to-nose and so tempting. "There's nobody out here. We can put your theory to the test, right here," she teased.

"It wouldn't be casual with us and you know it. That's where she got it wrong."

"So we couldn't be friends, and have an occasional turn in bed?"

Shocked she was actually proposing the idea, Gavin tread carefully. He'd like nothing more than to lay her bare on this blanket and bury himself inside her, but could he do that and walk away? Like it meant nothing? "No. I don't."

The sun, high in the sky, backlit her and made her glow like an angel. "Do you want more? Even after what happened?"

Gavin remembered how mean girl Jenny had gotten pictures of Gavin passed out in his dorm room bed. How she'd staged it to look like she'd been in the bed with him, and how she'd sent those pictures to Ally and his friends.

Gavin could never understand why Jenny thought that would make him change his mind about being with her, but in her twisted little brain, Ally was competition, and as long as she was out of the picture, that was all that mattered.

"You were just eighteen. And knowing you were insecure, I should have done more to convince you that you were the only girl I was interested in. She messed with your head."

Ally snuggled in. "I should have believed in you. I'm sorry I didn't."

"Why didn't you?" It came out before he could stop himself.

"I don't know. I wish I'd trusted you, talked to you about what happened. You'd never lied to me, or let me down. I should have had more faith. I was the one who let you down."

Locking his arms around her, he shook his head. "It's not all your fault. But hypothetically, if you had talked it out with me, what do you think would have happened between us?" Gavin knew what he thought. He was pretty well convinced they'd be married by now.

She hesitated, tears threatening. "I think we'd still be together. I wrecked everything."

Kissing her lightly, Gavin cursed himself. It was his pride and stubbornness that had kept him from going after Ally and helping her make sense out of the mess with Jenny.

"I think we're both to blame," he whispered into her hair. "You need to stop beating yourself up."

"You forgive me?" She sniffled, letting Gavin know she was crying.

"Yeah. I was angry at you for a day. After that, it was all on me. I should have come after you, but I didn't."

Tilting her face up, this time, Ally kissed him. She kissed him once, twice, three times. "We lost a lot of time," she said. "I'm scared to hope things could change, but at the same time, I'm scared to close the door on the possibilities."

He pulled her close, loving that finally, after all this time, he could. "You aren't alone."

Chapter Seven

TRUTHFULLY, ALLY DIDN'T know what to expect when she arrived at the guest ranch. The manager gave her early check-in so she could get plans unpacked, but the only thing she could think about was Gavin. As she and the staff member rode out to the glamping tent, with all her luggage and work paraphernalia, Ally was nursing a sliver of disappointment. The unique location and the romantic venue were going to be wasted on her and Gavin. Oh, sure. They would look like a couple, but their relationship was still confusing. On one hand, they had a hard time keeping their hands off each other, but there was also a healthy dose of caution to go along with it. They'd made progress, but Ally still didn't know where they were headed.

She'd been thinking about him constantly, especially since their heart-to-heart talk on their ride the day before. They'd agreed to keep things platonic for now, to take things slow, but Ally felt like she might actually have a second chance with Gavin, and that was kind of a miracle.

She'd missed him something awful. Granted, it was a good thing he wasn't around her first day at the ranch. He was way too tempting. But when he was there, something inside her just lit up. He was still the sweet guy she remembered from high school. But he definitely projected a harder edge now, even though his heart was all about helping others.

The man had always had nerves of steel. Ally remembered how terrifying it was to watch him deal with an out-of-control stallion, or climb into the rafters of the barn to rescue a cat. But at the heart of all that mettle was a heart of gold. That hadn't changed either.

He might affect the tough, unflappable persona, but on the inside, Gavin was a mush. Which was why she always loved him, and why she'd never stopped. His admission yesterday, that he was as much at fault as she was for their relationship going off the rails, gave her hope. She wasn't sure exactly what she was hoping for, but she felt happier than she had in years. Like maybe fate had called her home just at the right time.

The golf cart came to a halt in front of what appeared to be a pretty country cabin. It had a small porch with Adirondack chairs, pots filled with spring blooms and a view of the lake that was to die for.

"This is spectacular."

Following her escort inside, the place didn't disappoint. The inside of the cabin was outfitted for every comfort. A large comfortable sofa faced a stone fireplace, and rustic chic touches were everywhere. However, it was the bedroom that took Ally's breath away.

The threshold between the living room and the bedroom was where the transition from cabin to tent took place. The room was beautiful. The rough-hewn wood floor was covered by a red oriental rug, the furnishings were carefully selected, and the bed was the true crowning glory to the space. A large four-poster, it was high off the floor with a plush mattress, and what looked like a dozen pillows. It was covered in a gorgeous, soft flannel comforter in neutral hues, and crisp linens. There was a stove in the corner for warmth, a small table with a pair of chairs, and a bench that she was told contained extra blankets and towels.

Once she was left alone, Ally stood for a second and surveyed her space. The couple had made an excellent choice with this location. If Ally's accommodations were on the simpler side, she couldn't imagine what some of the luxury suites were like. She'd find out soon enough, as the majority of the wedding party and a good number of the guests were arriving later that afternoon.

Taking out her phone, Ally took a picture of the living room and sent it to Gavin.

Home Sweet Home, she captioned the picture.

Wow! That looks incredible!

It's gorgeous. I can't wait for you to see it.

Same. Be there tomorrow morning.

Tomorrow morning? She wasn't expecting him until later. She wondered if anything specific made him change his plans. Hopeful thoughts rushed through her head, and as quickly as they appeared, Ally tamped them down.

Yesterday was emotional; she couldn't afford to let her emotions get in the way of her judgment. If this was going to work out, there was no room for mistakes.

It would be so easy to be swept away by Gavin. At home, in a run-down gazebo, she almost lost control. On their ride in the country, she'd have done anything he asked. Here? In a perfect, dreamy location, with Montana's beauty as far as the eye could see? She was toast.

Walking into the bathroom, Ally gasped. It was opulent, with beautiful tile work, high-end fixtures, and a slant toward the romantic. This room had been built for two.

Staring at the oversized whirlpool tub and the huge shower with multiple spray heads, she uttered a prayer. "Lord, I am so screwed. Please give me strength."

Snapping her back to reality, Ally heard her phone ring. All she hoped was that it wasn't Gavin, or her mother. Picking it up off the bed, she saw it was Vivi. "Hey."

"Hey! Are you there? How is the place?"

"It's amazing," Ally said on a sigh. "It's really perfect."

"Will you have any free time? What kind of activities are there? When is Gavin arriving?" That was Vivi. All questions.

"Tomorrow morning. I think he's going to be pleasantly surprised."

Gavin had been expressing his doubts about the location, claiming it to be too good to be true. In some ways, Ally shared his doubts. The bride had booked the ranch before Ally's firm had been brought on board to plan the wedding. The place was closed over the winter for renovations, so she had never laid eyes on any of the spaces. Which made her very nervous.

But the staff she'd worked with remotely, from the reservations manager to the banquet director, had assured her she wouldn't be disappointed, and she wasn't.

"Are you going to be okay with this? With him so close all the time? I know it can't be easy."

"I'll be okay. I mean, we've come to an understanding. It's nice having my friend back."

Silence dropped between them, because Ally couldn't face the truth until Vivi forced her to.

"You've always wanted to be more than Gavin's friend. When are you going to stop kidding yourself, Al?"

Vivi's words went right to her heart. Yesterday sent her reeling. He could own her, heart and soul, which meant he could also break her. Did she give in and let the walls come down?

"I'm going to go. I promise I'll send lots of pictures."

"Ally," Vivi pleaded. "You can't ignore this."

"I'm not. We're not. We've been talking and coming to grips with what happened. We know there's a powerful attraction, and we're dealing. But it is between us. Okay? Look, I'll see you when I get back. I'll be at my parents for a day or two until I head back to Seattle."

"Fine. I think you're making a mistake." Vivi sounded hurt or worried. Maybe both.

"You don't know that. It's complicated."

"Hmm. Not really," Vivi replied before saying goodbye.

WHEN HE STOPPED his truck in front of the massive lodge, Gavin understood why Ally had told him the place was amazing. The building, which was a long, timber frame structure, had large windows, a porch that stretched the length of it, and welcomed guests in perfect mountain style. Turning, he checked out the property, which seemed to go on forever. He saw cabins and a colony of smaller buildings a little ways down the road, and he guessed that was where they were staying.

Yeah, *amazing* was a good word for this place. Greeted by a staff member who took his bag, and another who parked his truck for him, Gavin picked up on the luxury vibe. It was definitely more resort than ranch. As he walked into the soaring lobby, he heard Ally's familiar laughter. She was happy, and it was possible there was no better sound in the world. Following it, he found her in what looked like a ballroom. The ceilings were high, with beams creating the feel of a large barn, but a lot more refined. And clean.

She was talking to staff members about arrangements for the reception.

"Ma'am, if you want flowers over the rafters, we're going

to have to bring in the cherry picker for that."

"Well," Ally said with a smile, "It's a good thing you have one of those lovely contraptions. I'd hate to think you'd have to climb a rope to get up there."

The two men looked at each other, then tipped their hats in deference to the gorgeous redhead who had just told them sweetly, but in no uncertain terms, to get the job done.

That was pretty damn sexy.

Her authority was unchallenged. She was kind, respectful, but clear in what she wanted. As she walked with two other people to a large table where there were sketches and plans laid out, he couldn't help but love her confidence. It had become her most attractive feature.

Ally had always been beautiful; whatever she thought about her looks, she was a pretty teen who had grown into a knockout. But the game changer wasn't her weight or her clothes—it was how she felt about herself.

Gavin had nursed his broken heart for a good long time after Ally left him and Marietta behind, but now he could see she needed to leave. The town, as great as it was, would have kept Ally from being all she could be. She'd found her path, and had kicked ass. The woman was a fucking work of art.

Gavin had no intention of losing her again.

Pushing past him, a tall blond man strode into the room and straight for the table. "Ally! My God, it's good to see you! You look fantastic, darling."

Darling?

Ally turned, her face frozen, her smile obviously fake. "Hello, Lars."

Lars. The ex.

That was Gavin's cue. Pushing off the doorframe, he made his way to Ally, thinking about exactly how far he should take it. Subtle would be better, but kissing her senseless definitely had its appeal.

"Hey there, beautiful."

When Ally looked his way and smiled, for real, it felt like he'd been kicked in the chest. He'd do anything for her.

"Hi!" Walking away from Lars, Ally met him, stretching up on her tiptoes to kiss him. It was a simple kiss. Warm, familiar. The kiss of a lover. "I missed you."

The words could have been for show, but there was something very sincere and true about the look in her eyes.

"Missed you, too."

"Did you have a good drive up?"

"Uneventful. So, that's good in my book."

"I'm glad you're here," she said so quietly only he could hear.

"Is everything okay?"

Nodding, she pressed her head against his chest. "It is now."

There were words hanging between them. Words that would change everything.

"Ally, you have a new guy," Lars said. "Wow. Unexpected."

"Uh, yes." She stepped back, smoothing her shirt. "Lars Sundstrom, this is Gavin Clark."

"Gavin, a pleasure." Lars extended his hand and they shook. "So how did you and Ally meet?"

Yeah, he didn't like this asswipe already. "We've known each other for years. Grew up together."

"Is that so? You're from that little town, Marichetta?"

Marichetta? Was this guy for real? "Marietta. Yes."

"Wow." Lars folded his arms and tucked his hands into his armpits. "Are you a cowboy? I've never met one."

Ally was about to say something, but this was too good. He squeezed her hand and stopped her. Gavin figured the idiot would hang himself eventually, and Gavin had no problem handing him some rope. "I grew up on a ranch, yes sir."

"Amazing. Such a different life. I've always lived in cities. Grew up in LA. You know, in California."

"I've heard of it," Gavin said flatly. Lars thought he was stupid, which should have pissed Gavin off, but he was mildly amused instead. Ally, on the other hand, was mortified.

"I'm going to go settle into the room," he said to Ally, ignoring the asshole. "Why don't you meet me there when you're free."

"I just have a few more things to finalize, then I'll be there. We can take a ride later on."

Lars clapped his hands together. "That would be great! I'll get Jasmina and we'll all go."

That would spoil the plan in about a dozen different ways, not the least of which was that he and Ally wouldn't be alone. Their time together two days ago was seared in his brain. This time, if he got her out in a secluded pasture, he was going to take advantage of it.

"Lars, Gavin and I want to go out on our own. You and Jasmina wouldn't be able to keep up."

"Keep up? How hard can it be? You just sit in the saddle."

Ally shook her head in disbelief. "Harder than it looks. I'll see you later at the rehearsal."

Damn, she got a gold star for that one. Gavin kissed her once more for good measure and let go of her hand. "See you at the cabin. Take care, Olaf."

Gavin turned on his booted heel and left the room with Lars sputtering something about his name. The guy was such a dick. Ally was lucky he moved on, and Gavin had every intention of showing her she had better options.

ALLY ALMOST RAN back to the cabin; she couldn't wait to kiss Gavin for real. He evoked a sparkly, giddy feeling way deep down in her belly, and no matter how much Ally tried to deny it, it was there.

When she walked in the front room, she saw Gavin

WEEKEND WITH HER BACHELOR

standing in front of the long sofa, examining it.

"What's wrong?"

He was annoyed and she had no idea why. "It's not a pull-out."

It took Ally a second to process what he said. Originally, she'd planned on walking in here and kissing him senseless. But now, once it clicked, she understood. No sofa bed.

"No?"

"Nope. It's fine. I can sleep on the couch."

Taking a long look at the sofa that would undoubtedly kill his back, Ally stepped into him. "I don't think that's necessary. We can share."

"Ally, that's asking for trouble." His eyes went dark and stormy. "The way things have been going…"

"I trust you," she said, cutting him off. It was the only reassurance she had. "I trust our friendship."

He did not look convinced. "I dunno."

"It's a big bed, Gavin."

He ran his hand up her arm, setting off tingles all over her body and alarm bells in her head. Oh, boy.

Maybe her suggestion wasn't so smart. There was electricity surrounding them, and when he brushed his lips against her ear, she moaned. Just a little bit. God, she was weak.

"It's the things I want to do to you in that big bed that make this a problem," he said. "I dream about touching you, kissing you everywhere, and making love to you until you scream my name, Allison."

"Oh, my God…" She could feel him. All he'd done was whisper the words to her and she could imagine it—every touch, every kiss, every sensation. It made her lightheaded.

Stepping back, he raised an eyebrow. "Still want to risk it? The couch is safer."

"You'll be uncomfortable. You're so big." Gavin was almost six-four and over two hundred pounds. Ally, who wasn't short by any standard, felt dwarfed by him. Thinking of him crammed on the couch just seemed wrong.

"I'll manage. You said you trust me? Then trust me about this."

Ally broke away, more disappointed than annoyed and grabbed her riding clothes before heading to the bathroom to change. "I'll be right out."

Once the door was closed, Ally sank to the floor and cursed herself. She was all over the place about the possibility of getting into a relationship with Gavin. Her heart wanted him in a life changing way, but his response to her offer to just share the bed forced her to see that while he wanted her, he still wasn't sure of her. Of them.

She took a deep breath, gathered her thoughts, and reminded herself she shouldn't be surprised. There was a great affection between them, but the trust issues ran deep. Something was still holding him back.

That's it. No crime. Nothing unexpected, if she was honest with herself. Just the realization that, once again, she was blinded by the idea of romance.

Coming into this situation, Ally had a very specific need. To unload the ring, to donate some money, and to have a fun date for the wedding.

She'd accomplished all those goals.

That should have been enough.

It never would be.

Chapter Eight

G AVIN WOKE TO Ally's voice coming from the bedroom. He'd spent a restless night on the couch, trying to get comfortable in a space that was not made for someone his size. Ally was right on that point; he was too big.

Unlike her conversation with the French maître d', Ally's voice was calm and relaxed. She was discussing a morning-after breakfast for the wedding guests, and all the talk about food was making him hungry. Sitting up, he glanced around for his hoodie and threw it on before walking to the front door.

He could feel the chill in the air before he even stepped outside. It was a typical spring morning in the mountains. Not quite freezing, the air would warm as the day went on. It was almost May, and it looked like the bride and groom would get terrific weather for their wedding.

In the crisp morning, delicious aromas from the lodge carried on the air, and Gavin's stomach really started to yell when he smelled breakfast. He couldn't wait anymore. It was time to grab Ally and head to the lodge. They had a long day ahead and both of them needed to eat.

Poking his head into the bedroom, he didn't think he'd ever seen a prettier woman in the morning. Ally was sitting up in bed, covers to her waist, going over her planner. The room was bathed in morning sunlight, and the entire space glowed from it. All he could see she was wearing was a soft pink T-shirt which outlined every curve, and her hair was pulled into a messy ponytail. She wore no makeup, and a pair of glasses were perched on her nose. Every nerve ending fired when he looked at her.

Something must have broken her concentration, because she looked up, flashing a brilliant smile when she saw him. "Morning. How did you sleep?"

"It could have been better," he said entering the room. "How about you?"

"Okay. I never sleep well in strange beds."

If he hadn't been an idiot about sharing the bed, they both might have slept better. "Do you want to get some breakfast?"

"Sure. I showered last night, so why don't you use the bathroom while I get dressed."

If she was bothered about their conversation yesterday, she didn't show it, but Ally was always good at hiding her feelings. A problem, in his mind. She shouldn't have to hide that big heart from anyone. Especially him.

"Okay. Let me get my clothes."

Ally tossed back the covers and he saw her T-shirt was the only thing she was wearing. It hit at mid-thigh, showing off her long, shapely legs. Gavin wondered what the hell was wrong with him that he hadn't slept with this woman. Why hadn't he chased her down years ago, and struggled to make things work?

She stood and stretched her arms over her head, causing her T-shirt to ride up, stopping just before the Promised Land. Ally was either oblivious to him, or she was torturing him deliberately. Either way he was in trouble.

And his dick got hard the minute she stepped into his space.

"Are you all right?" she wondered. "You look, I don't know, annoyed."

"I'm not annoyed."

"No?" She stretched up and kissed him on the cheek. "Okay. Go get ready. Now that you mentioned breakfast, I'm hungry."

"Right." Grabbing his underwear and jeans, he headed into the shower. It was going to be a cold one.

ALLY HEARD THE shower go off and thought about Gavin, dripping wet just beyond the door. Her body responded just thinking about him. Last night before they went to sleep, she'd seen him with his shirt off, top button of his jeans popped, muscles defined… she could barely breathe. He was gorgeous, and sadly, her mother wasn't wrong. She really needed to get laid.

That the only person she wanted to be with wasn't sure he wanted her was a problem. Looking around the dresser, she couldn't find her mascara, and remembered she'd left it on the bathroom counter.

Oh, darn.

Wearing nothing but a pretty, lacy, button down tunic shirt over her lingerie, she knocked on the door. Who needed jeans? They were just friends.

"Gavin, are you decent?"

"Yeah, kind of." Opening the door, he stood there with a towel wrapped around his waist and his face covered in shaving cream. There was a strip of dark hair running from the center of his chest, over his belly and into the towel. How she wasn't throwing herself at him, she didn't know. Gavin was more man that Lars had ever been.

"Sorry, but the light's better in here and I have to do my makeup. Do you mind?"

He looked her up and down, stopping right where her tunic brushed against her thighs. "No pants?"

"Not yet. Is that a problem?"

"No," he said while stepping back to let her in. "No problem."

Ally grinned as she went by, happy that it was clearly a problem. Standing beside each other, he shaved as she did her makeup.

Looks passed between them in the mirror. Flirty glances. Grins. Some grumbles from him here and there. Annoying him had never been so much fun.

"That looks like a lot of work," he growled. "All the paint."

"It's not really. I mean, I don't wear much and I'm used to it, so it doesn't take very long."

He nodded, drawing the blade slowly around his chin. Ally had always wondered why her mother liked to watch her father shave, and now as she kept a close eye on Gavin, she understood. There was something very sexy about it. Slow. Steady. Masculine.

When he'd finished, Gavin's eyes locked with hers as he grabbed a towel and wiped the little remnants of shaving cream off his face. At the same time, Ally pulled out her pony tail and started fluffing her curls.

Surprised, Ally froze when he reached out and took a wavy strand between his fingers and wound it up.

"It's beautiful," he said.

Ally's heart was thumping in her chest, staring at Gavin while he examined her hair. "Thank you. I've learned to accept it for what it is."

"You're beautiful. All of you."

She couldn't help herself; Ally reached out and touched his freshly shaved cheek. His eyes drifted shut as he took her hand, dropping soft kisses on all her knuckles. Then, Gavin opened his eyes, and in them she saw her deepest feelings. Her most secret desires.

"Yes," she whispered. "Yes."

"Are you sure?" His large hands were cradling her face now, gentle and strong. Hers. He was hers.

Nodding, she reached between them and undid his towel, letting it fall to the floor.

He was a work of art. Muscular without being bulky. But it was the man inside with whom she had fallen in love. Being able to admit that to herself, even if she couldn't admit it to him, was a milestone of sorts. If she'd faced it when she was eighteen, trusted in him, they might never have been apart.

He'd been working the buttons on her shirt with his big hands, watching it fall open a little at a time. Once he was done, he pushed it off her shoulders, letting it fall into a puddle next to his towel on the floor.

Hoping they might get here, Ally had put on her prettiest bra and thong. Not taking his eyes off hers, Gavin's fingers brushed over the swell of her breasts, grazed her ribs, and skimmed across her belly. He touched her gently, thoughtfully.

"You're perfect, Ally. But do we really want to do this?"

"Let's not think about anything but today. We'll deal with whatever comes when we get home. But let's accept that there's some kind of magic going on here, Gavin. We've always had magic."

"I know." In one motion, Gavin lifted her into the safety of his arms, kissing her while he carried her to the warmth of the big bed. A bed they would finally share.

Wasting no time, because they'd done too much of that already, he undid the front clasp on her bra and pushed it aside. The cool air hitting her nipples made them pebble and peak. He smiled and nipped the sensitive tip, making her arch.

"Ah, that's how it is?" He smiled down at her, so handsome her heart was skipping beats. "This is going to be fun."

"Fun?" Ally had had her share of great sex. It was pleasurable, and provided release. But she'd never had *fun* in bed. Maybe that was part of the problem.

"Uh huh. And you remember that screaming my name thing from yesterday? Get yourself ready."

His hands were sliding over her hips, tugging down her thong. She could only imagine what he had in mind. Gavin hovered over her, fully erect, and Ally had a little bit of anxiety thinking about everything this represented. Sex would change everything between them.

"Quiet your mind, Ally. We'll be okay."

"We will?"

"Yes." His mouth came down over hers, taking her away in a kiss that was gentle, sweet, possessive. She cherished the way he made her feel protected. *Loved.* She tasted his essence, strong and kind.

And as his lips and tongue moved over her body, nipping at her neck and shoulders, teasing her breasts, sucking each until she felt an ache low in her belly, she whispered, "Oh, God…"

He didn't stop, shackling her hands above her head. "You're so beautiful, Ally, and I'm going to have you every way I can."

"Mmm. I sure hope so."

KISSING HER BELLY, Gavin worked his way down, reveling in the smooth skin and sweet smell. They shouldn't be doing this, but nothing mattered more than making her happy. And if he got her to scream his name in the process, that was a win.

But Ally seemed to have another idea, as she scooted out from under him, kneeling and waiting for him. She looked like a goddess with her full breasts, gorgeous curves, and long hair curling down to her waist. There was magic between them all right, and it was all her.

Staring at her, he had no idea what she was up to. "Ally, get back here."

"Hmmm. Make me."

It wasn't hard. His hand shot around her, and coming down flat on her back, he hauled her back to him. "Now, I have something I have to do."

"Gavin. Come on. Please."

Separating her legs with his hands, Gavin looked up into Ally's face. She was sitting against the headboard, a combination of apprehensive and eager, and she could see exactly what he was doing. Gavin had every intention of blowing her mind. He didn't go in with his mouth, but with his fingers. He stroked and teased, watching her body respond.

She was warm and wet, and his finger had no trouble slipping inside her. The penetration surprised her, but the little turn of her lips let him know she was just fine.

Taking advantage, a second finger went in and he worked them, teasing her unfairly. Her hips moved slowly in a steady rhythm, allowing, and when Gavin withdrew his hand, he pressed her knees apart and started assaulting her with his mouth.

He licked her warm folds, sucked her, nibbled, and teased, but no how much she begged and cried out, he kept it up. She was amazing. "Oh, Gavin!"

Gavin's dick was so hard he thought he might explode. Moving back up her body, the tip teased her, and with each drop of wetness, he was closer to being very embarrassed.

Her hands came down and gripped his hips, bringing him closer. They were both on the edge, and the thought of coming with her wrapped around him proved to be the breaking point. Gavin started to enter her.

"I need you inside me," she begged.

He pushed deeper, seating himself a little at a time. She was tight and wet, but considering the blissful smile on her face and the mischief in her eyes, Ally was doing just fine.

"God," she cried out. "More, Gavin."

"I could hurt you."

"You won't..." Ally stroked his face with such tenderness. "I know you won't."

With her legs wrapped around him, her hips thrusting so hard, he couldn't hold back. Finally, Gavin drove into her, making love to the amazing woman he was destined to be with.

"Ally." She consumed him, body and soul. Made his mind cloud and his heart feel full. There was a primal need overwhelming him, basic and proprietary. Ally was his woman. His match. His mate.

Moving, they instantly caught the other's rhythm, their bodies in perfect sync. Fearing he might crush her, Gavin slipped his hands under her back and rolled them, so she was on top. Ally lifted her head and smiled.

"Smooth move, Clark," she teased.

"I got a million of 'em."

It was Ally's turn to take control. Straddling him, she started to move. Gavin gripped her hips to steady her as she caught a wave of sensation and brought them both to the edge. Her face was content, beautiful, and her body was lush, soft, warm… a woman's body. The body of a woman who could be the mother of his children. A woman he wanted to grow old with.

The fever between them built, with Ally moving harder and faster, her eyes closed, her head thrown back from the sensations. Gavin felt the tightness in his groin, the wave as nerve endings fired. He was trying to hold on until she came…

And then she did. Crying out, arching, Gavin finally let go, emptying himself in her. She contracted around him, milking him. Her body, her heart, her soul owned him.

Ally collapsed on his chest, their bodies sticking together, out of breath and shuddering with aftershocks.

"Christ," was the only thing he was able to utter.

"Mmmm." She was purring like a kitten. "That was amazing. You're amazing."

"Jesus, we're really good together." Knowing that now was going to make parting even more difficult. But there was something else on his mind as he thought about cleaning up. "I didn't use anything," he said quietly.

Eyes wide, she stared at him. "Damn."

"I mean, I'm sure it's fine. You're on the pill, aren't you?"

Rolling off of him, Ally laid next to him on the bed. "I've been off for about six months. Wanted to give my body a break."

"Ah. Okay." He paused. She could be... "We should be fine, right?"

"You're the doctor. You tell me."

Ally rose, heading straight to the bathroom, and if he didn't know her better he would have sworn she slammed the door.

No, she did slam the door.

That made perfect sense. Have mind-blowing sex. Get pissed off.

"Ally?" No answer. "Ally? What's wrong?"

"Nothing."

Nothing. That was right up there with *fine.*

"Baby, toss me a towel, okay?"

A minute went by when she finally opened the door. As she stormed by, makeup reapplied, hair fixed, she threw a towel right in his face. When she went for her bra and panties, Gavin grabbed her wrist and pulled her back into bed.

"Tell me what's wrong."

She struggled as he pinned her to the mattress. "You have no right to do this to me. Let me up!"

"Not until you tell me what's set you off."

She turned her head to the side, angry and proud. He couldn't resist kissing her long, lovely neck. "Tell me."

"No." Her voice came out on a breath.

"I can't apologize and mean it if you don't tell me." He kept kissing her, moving to her collarbone. "Please tell me."

Trailing his lips in a line down her chest, Gavin traveled between her breasts while he laced his fingers with hers. She wasn't struggling anymore. Instead, her body was moving under the attention he was giving her, inviting him back into her warmth.

"I wouldn't try to trap you," she said so softly he could barely hear.

"Oh, Ally. I know that. If anything happens, we're in this together."

Freeing her hands, Ally brought her fingers to his cheeks and guided his mouth to hers. This kiss was sweet, loving, beautiful. It was the kiss a future was built upon. Feeling her legs wrap around his waist, Gavin slipped inside her.

There was nothing frantic or urgent about coming together this time, this was him making love to his best friend. The girl—*the woman*—who had the power to change his life.

Chapter Nine

"SO WHO ARE the bride and groom?" Gavin asked.

Ally tilted her head to far side of the dining room, where a round table was filled with all her friends from Seattle. "Cindy and Rajiv. They're in the corner. Cindy is a nurse practitioner and Raj is a software developer. They're really adorable together."

She saw Lars at the table, and held Gavin's hand even tighter. They were the last ones in for breakfast, and considering the two amazing orgasms he'd given her, Ally was amazed she hadn't fallen right to sleep.

"Is that Olaf's shield maiden?"

Gavin hadn't given up on Lars' nickname, and Ally had to admit, it was funny. Next to him was Jasmina, the woman with whom he'd cheated. Thin and willowy, with super-short blonde hair, Ally still got angry looking at her. The only thing in front of her was an apple and a bottle of water. "Yup. That's her."

"She looks unhappy."

"I think she's unimpressed. Can't be bothered."

Gavin spun her into his arms and kissed her soundly.

"Maybe that will impress her."

"Hmm." Ally kissed him again. "I don't know about her, but it sure impresses me."

He smiled and the entire room just lit up. Talk about blindsided. With Gavin around, Ally felt like a teenager again. Only better.

Walking through the busy dining room, Ally and Gavin almost tripped over a little boy who was racing around the tables at light speed. He might have been three years old.

Gavin did what came naturally and scooped the little guy up just before he took out an elderly gentleman with a cane.

"Hey there, buddy. You can't go running around tables like that, you'll get yourself hurt."

"Hey! Hey you! Give me my son." A petite brunette charged Gavin and yanked the child out of his arms. "Who do you think you are, snatching him up like that? He doesn't know you."

"I'm sorry, ma'am, but I was trying to keep him from getting hurt."

"I was watching. He was fine."

"Oh, you were?" Gavin raised an eyebrow, but realized quickly the woman wasn't going to listen. "All right then."

Ally was stunned at the woman's rude behavior. "Ma'am, are you a wedding guest?"

"Yes. I work with Raj." She didn't introduce herself; obviously she was too important for that.

"Nice to meet you. I'm Ally Beaumont, the event planner."

Brunette put her child down and he took off like a shot. This kid was a toddling lawsuit. "I hope the other guests have a better understanding of limits," she snapped.

But before Ally could tell her to keep her little boy under control, there was a loud crash and a scream. Wonderboy had made impact.

"Jace! Oh, no." Brunette went screaming at a server who was sitting on the floor, food everywhere, and the toddler was crying hysterically. Gavin was at the boy's side before anyone else was close. "You idiot! What did you do to my son?"

Ignoring the mother's screeching, Gavin eased the little boy onto his back. "Hey, pal. What happened?"

All Ally heard was a blood-curdling scream. Then the kid's mother started alternately berating Gavin and the server, who was being tended to by his boss.

"Ally, I need ice, a few soft towels and some gauze." Gavin was calmly assessing the child while chaos surrounded him. This was what he did. Who he was.

Simply put, he was amazing.

Lars had walked over and folded his arms, his usual arrogant stance. "Hey, Cowboy. Shouldn't you wait for the professionals to take care of the kid?"

Gavin rolled his eyes and ignored Lars, paying attention to young Jace instead.

"Lars, don't worry your little head. Gavin is a doctor,"

Ally responded before turning to the mother, who was enraged. "He's an emergency physician. Your son is in good hands." She almost said something snotty about the mother not watching the child, but didn't think she should add fuel to the fire. Although it was tempting. The woman was not a nice person.

Cindy had gone to help the server, who had a few cuts that needed cleaning, and by the time the ambulance arrived, the wounds and injuries had been tended to. Jace was splinted with some plush towels, and the server was going to be fine but needed to be checked at the ER.

The screaming mother was quiet, but didn't say thank you. Lars had been put in his place, and Ally couldn't have been more proud of Gavin, or more proud to be with him. It was one thing to know what he did; it was another to see him in action. Most beautiful was the way he handled the little boy.

He'd be a great father someday.

Once the commotion settled down, Cindy, the bride, sidled up to Ally gave her a poke in the ribs. "He's fantastic," she said referring to Gavin. "What a doll."

"He really is."

"Lars is dying over there; he's so jealous. Jasmina hasn't given him the time of day and you're with Dr. All-American Boy."

"I'm just trying to be happy. Lars isn't a consideration." God. Ally was going to go to hell for the lies she was telling.

She was thrilled Lars was bothered. Although, since things had changed between her and Gavin, maybe she wasn't lying quite so much.

Gavin came up behind her and took her hand like he had every right. After exchanging a few pleasantries with the bride, he led her to a corner table that had been set with a basket of warm muffins and a pot of hot coffee.

Once seated, Gavin scanned the menu. "I'm starved."

She nodded, unable to speak, because she realized she had a big problem where he was concerned. How would she manage without him? She didn't want to find out, but could they have a future?

"Me too." She paused and looked up at him. "You were great with Jace. Really."

"He's a cute kid, but he's out of control. Mom was telling me they've banned the word 'no' so he doesn't feel stifled."

"He's just a little boy." Ally couldn't believe it.

"I told her an occasional 'no' isn't going to stifle anything and will keep him safe. He's too young to have control. She wasn't having any of it."

"Well, you did your part. That's all you can do."

He nodded. They ordered a huge farm breakfast of pancakes, eggs and bacon, and Ally settled back in her seat with her coffee to watch the world go by.

"I... I like kids," Gavin stammered.

His statement came out of the blue. She never doubted

that he liked kids, so she wondered what drove him to mention it. Jace, possibly, but she had the feeling there was something else. "Okay. Me too."

"If you were, you know, pregnant, I think we'd be okay. Once we decided on where we'd live."

Where they would live? Ally was overwhelmed and thrilled at the same time. He was offering marriage if their carelessness produced a child. It wasn't even a question. Maybe the independent woman in her should be offended, but she wasn't. She just loved him a little more.

"Gavin, chances are nothing is going to happen. I love that you're trying to reassure me, but I don't think we're going to have to worry about it."

"You're right," he said on a nervous laugh. "I know that, but I guess I was thinking that I wouldn't mind it so much. You know, having a baby. With you." His big hand took hold of hers. "I have no idea what made me say that. I'm sorry."

What happened to the quiet, staid alpha guy? The strong, silent type? "You're confusing me. That's all."

The waiter placed their overflowing breakfasts in front of them. It all looked really good.

"I'm sure. I don't know what made me say that. I guess… I don't know."

"Who knows why we say certain things." She poked at her eggs. "It's a nice thought, though. Being parents."

"Yeah. It is."

GAVIN LAY ON the bed in the room, thinking about all the things that had transpired so far that day. Talk about one for the books. Ally was at the location where the wedding ceremony was going to take place, dealing with last minute details. He wanted to talk to her, but he just didn't know if there would be time.

She could be pregnant. And what floored him about the idea was that he didn't hate it. In fact, he liked it. A lot. Mostly because it meant he could keep Ally. Which was the wrong reason for wanting a kid.

This truly sucked.

When she rolled back in his life, Gavin never expected Ally to affect him like this. All he wanted to do was avoid complications. There were so many things wrong with their relationship, not the least of which was the distance. They didn't live in the same place, and unless one of them made a big change, it didn't look like they were going to.

The thing was, he was considering it. If she wanted it, he might move to Seattle and get a job there. Gavin just didn't want to lose her again.

Outside, the sound of a golf cart pulling up in front of the cabin let him know she was back. It didn't take long for Ally to fly into the bedroom and fall face first onto the mattress.

"I am so tired."

"Do you have time for a nap?" he asked.

"Not really." Scooting herself up on the bed, Ally grabbed a pillow and turned on her side, facing him. "I have to get dressed soon. So much to do. But the bride looks stunning! I saw her a few minutes ago." She was giddy over the plans coming together. He knew she'd been working hard on this event.

"I'm sure she's beautiful." He paused. "You really love your work, don't you?"

She smiled. "It can be very stressful, but yeah. I really do. It's happy work."

He didn't know if he should do this, but he wanted to know where they stood. "Have you ever thought of basing your business in Montana?"

Ally froze and looked him in the eyes. "I haven't, why?"

"I don't know. I just thought we might be able to make a go of this if you were closer."

"Much of my business is based in the city. I don't know if it would survive a move like that."

"Right. Sure."

"I mean I love home, but... it would be a huge change."

"Yeah, it would. I guess I just wanted to float it out there."

He waited. She didn't say anything. Didn't ask him if he would consider moving.

Her silence spoke volumes. Maybe this was really a friends with benefits arrangement, nothing more, and Ally hadn't realized it.

"Are you angry, Gavin?"

Sitting up, he tried not to react. He couldn't, because he already felt like a fucking idiot. "What time do we have to be there?"

"We have a little time. A couple of hours, at least. Why aren't you talking about this? I didn't realize me moving was something that had to be considered."

"It's not. Don't worry about it. I had a thought, that was all."

The way her brows furrowed let him know she wasn't quite buying it. "If you say so."

"It's good." He stood and stepped away from the bed. "I'm going to take a shower, unless you need to go first."

Crawling across the bed, Ally knelt up and placed her hands on his chest, her lips curling into a kittenish smile. "We could share a shower. Yes?"

He wanted nothing more than to take her. To bury himself in all that warm, wet heat. But he couldn't right now. He had to draw the line someplace.

"If I get you in that shower, you aren't going to be able to walk later."

"There's some appeal to that, you know? What does that tell you?"

He kissed her lightly. "That you really like sex."

"I like sex with you," she purred. "Come on, Gavin. Let's take a shower."

She was like a siren drawing him in. Her lips skimmed

his jaw, teasing a response, and his sharp intake of breath gave her exactly what she wanted.

"You're going to be the death of me, Ally. I swear," he growled.

"Nah. This is going to be fun. I can't wait to hear you scream." She was a tease of the highest order.

"I'm not a screamer," he said flatly. "But you are welcome to try."

With that, he wrapped his arms around her waist and lifted her, walking the short distance to the bathroom. Ally was already stripping her clothes off as he carried her—her top and bra went first, then she started working the buttons on his shirt.

Once her feet hit the floor, she went right for the button of his jeans.

"You are impatient," he said. As angry as he was feeling, he was at her mercy—whatever she wanted. So if this was it for them, Gavin was going to make sure he rocked her world.

But Ally was being pretty damn aggressive; she was in nothing but a thong while she yanked his jeans and briefs down. He was hard as a rock, and moaned as Ally stroked him from his balls to the tip.

"Don't run away," she cooed. Stepping back, she leaned into the shower and turned on the multiple sprays. "Now, what should we do first?"

"You are shameless." Gavin had never been with a woman like her. The confidence, the knowledge of what she wanted, was a major turn-on. She pressed her body to his, her hands grazing a path down his sides. He was all hers. Even if he didn't want to be. Even knowing he may never see her after the weekend. He was hers.

"I want you, Gavin. I want to take you inside me. Feel you move. Be close."

"You have me, all of me."

The shower jets soaked them as soon as they stepped in the tiled space, raining down on their bodies like a summer storm. The feelings churning inside them were as tumultuous as a heaving ocean, all consuming and wickedly dangerous.

He kissed her, holding Ally as close as he could, until their bodies almost melted together.

Gavin never thought much about his heart. He was about his work, about his family. He wasn't an emotional guy. But with Ally, he felt everything. He wanted a life that had her in it, but if he couldn't have that, he'd take the now. He'd make her feel what he felt.

In a move that made her breath catch, Gavin lifted her up, pressing her back to the wall, and slowly lowered her down onto his erection. He watched her face as he entered her, the bliss, the pleasure, washing over her.

It was beautiful. She was beautiful, and for a little while longer, she was his.

Chapter Ten

THERE WAS NOTHING like a ride in a horse-drawn carriage. It was especially nice when the carriage dropped you off at your door after a really great party. Ally was giddy with happiness. The wedding was her most successful yet; the guests had had an amazing time, and the bride and groom had the memory of a lifetime.

On top of it all, the resort wanted to contract with her to be their official event planner. It appeared Ally would be spending more time in Montana after all, so maybe moving wasn't so far fetched.

Now she could crawl into bed besides the most hand-some date ever, celebrate with a bottle of very expensive champagne she'd grabbed from the bar, and then fall blissful-ly to sleep.

Ally had some details to finish up after the party broke up, and sent Gavin back to the cabin with a kiss and a thank you. Just being with him had made the whole weekend better. Now they had another full day together to sleep late, make love, and enjoy this amazing place before heading back to civilization. She couldn't wait to tell him about the offer from the resort.

Lars had asked about the engagement ring before he left the reception, and all Ally told him was that she donated the money she got for the ring to a great charity. She also informed him where he could buy the ring back if that's what he really wanted. Ironic, that the ring that tied her to another man had brought her such happiness with another.

She never seen a man in a huff, but Lars stormed off like a hormonal thirteen-year-old girl. It made her giggle a bit. What a jerk. He deserved everything he got. Karma was definitely biting him in the ass.

Oddly, Gavin's truck was parked outside the cabin, and for a second she wondered why. Walking up the steps and into the main room, she stopped short, dropping her shoes, when she saw Gavin's duffle packed and sitting on the couch.

Going to the bedroom, he was sitting on the edge of the bed in jeans and a soft grey Henley. He wasn't climbing into bed with her. The truck. The bag. It was obvious: he was leaving.

"You want to tell me what's going on?" Shit. Her voice was shaking. "Why is your bag packed?"

He rose, the look on his face telling her there was no use in arguing. "I'm heading out. I figure with the roads quiet, I can get back to Bozeman in a couple of hours."

"Why are you leaving?"

He stuffed his hands in his pockets. "I think you know

why."

"No, I don't know," she snapped. "I have no idea. Obviously you didn't tell me the truth today when I asked what was wrong. Is that what we're doing now, playing a guessing game?"

"I'm not going to cry about my feelings, Ally," he snarled. "I have some pride. You're not into this relationship the same way I am. I thought you were, but I was wrong. Fine. We'll move on."

"What are you talking about? I'm not into it? I love you. I love you so much it hurts."

He froze at her declaration. Softening for a second, but then seeming to shake it off.

"We can't do this long distance," he said, "no matter how we feel about each other. You know it. But you're content with the life you have in the city, and that's fine."

"So that's it. No conversation, no discussion. You've made the decision and we're over."

She walked into the living room and looked out the large front window. It was so dark; the sky was a blanket of stars. She'd never have this view in Seattle. Never have it anywhere but home. Gavin's hands settled on her shoulders. "We never even got started, Al. Isn't it best to cut our losses?"

"I don't understand. Is it because I said I couldn't move? I didn't say no. Just that it would be difficult."

"That's true, but you didn't seem too keen on the idea, and I'm not begging."

"Begging. Discussing something is begging now. Okay. You know, Gavin, I didn't hear you say anything about moving to the city. It was all about me moving back to Montana."

"You never *asked* me to move. I want you as part of my life, Ally. Do you want me in yours? That *discussion* goes both ways."

Boom. Had she really not said anything?

Never in her life had she felt such pressure in her chest. The pain was so raw, so acute, she could barely breathe. But was she supposed to be a mind reader now? Could he just walk away, knowing she wanted to be with him? Knowing she loved him? If he did, then he wasn't who she thought he was.

"Go," she squeaked out. "Just go."

"Ally, I'm sorry, but this is better for both of us."

"If you say so." She didn't even bother telling him the good news about the resort. It didn't matter anymore. "Drive safe."

He didn't offer any more explanations, or excuses. Gavin placed his cowboy hat on his head, put on his jacket, and grabbed his duffle. They parted when he dropped a kiss on her cheek, but Ally didn't move. She didn't even watch him leave the cabin.

The engine of the big Ford roared to life, and when he pulled away she could follow the tail lights as the truck made its way down the road. Once it had vanished from sight, Ally locked the door and grabbed the champagne, figuring getting drunk was the only thing left to do. But suddenly, the bedroom felt wrong without him there. Empty. Sad. They'd thoroughly enjoyed each other the last few days, and now just like that, it was over.

"I don't understand, Gavin," she mumbled before taking a long sip of the champagne right from the bottle. "You could have told me."

Running through the day in her head, she tried to think of the point when their relationship shifted. She remembered when he asked her about moving her business; he didn't exactly ask her to uproot her whole life. But he was right, she didn't invite him to be part of hers. She'd never even put that out there.

He could have mentioned it on his own. Made the offer. But would he have done that without an opening from her? This weekend had been all about her life, her people. Never once had she thought about how, or if, Gavin might fit in.

Of course, he was charming and fun at the wedding. Everyone loved him; hands down, she always had her best time when Gavin was involved.

She assumed, foolishly, that everything would fall into place.

The problem was he was the only one talking about how to make it work.

"He could have mentioned it," she said aloud, drinking more. "Men. Pssht. Maybe I'll just get a cat. *Or ten.*"

It was stupid of her to be mad, because Gavin wouldn't have brought it up. He never would have assumed anything, or pushed a point. He respected her too much to insert himself into her life without hearing from her first that he was welcome there.

A respectful man. Just her luck.

It had been her move, her chance to help them find their future, and she'd bungled it. She screwed up a chance at true happiness—again. He was the only man she wanted to be with. The only one.

After another long pull from the bottle, Ally felt her eyes burn. One tear came, and then another and another. She didn't even try to stop them.

She'd made a mess of everything, and that realization is what did it. The floodgates opened and Ally sobbed, as her heart shattered into a million pieces.

HE DIDN'T GO to Bozeman. Gavin drove straight home.

Pulling down the driveway of the ranch, he saw light was just breaking over the horizon. Some horses were already turned out in the big pasture along the drive, a sure sign that the farm was awake.

Pulling into his spot near the house, there was light in the kitchen, meaning his mother was up. He didn't know if he was ready for the questions she was going to ask, but if nothing else, he could use a big breakfast and a strong cup of coffee.

God, he felt like shit. And it had nothing to do with driving all night. He kept seeing Ally, standing in her sparkly dress, her back to him, strong and resolved. And hurt. He'd done that, and he wasn't very proud of it.

Grooms and hands were laughing over hot coffee and muffins, and he heard the neighs and whinnies of horses in the distance. It was familiar. Comforting. The sounds of morning on the farm hadn't changed in forever.

Walking into the kitchen, he was assaulted by the smell of bacon, sausage, and breakfast potatoes. There was warm, fresh bread still steaming on the counter, and looking around for signs of life, only his mother sat at the kitchen table scanning something on her tablet.

"Hi, Mom."

"Gavin! What on earth! I didn't expect to see you for a few weeks, at least."

She rose and hugged him, sensing immediately that there was something wrong. "Hmmm," she said, examining his face. "Sit down. I'll fix you something to eat. Coffee?"

"Definitely." He could use a good strong cup. His head was starting to hurt from the lack of sleep.

They didn't talk for a few minutes. Instead, his mother fried up a couple of eggs and loaded them on a plate with bacon, potatoes, and some bread with jam. Refilling both his coffee and her own, Mom sat across from him and watched him eat. It wasn't unusual; she often said one of her greatest pleasures in life was feeding her family.

"So," she began. "What did you do?"

Gavin froze, a piece of bread just grazing his lips. "What do you mean?"

"Don't be obtuse, Gavin. You're here because something happened with Ally. So I'm asking. What did you do?"

"Why are you assuming it was me?"

"Because you don't look angry, you look like you lost your best friend."

That's exactly what happened. But facing it, and his role in it, wasn't easy. "I let my fool pride get in the way of the best thing that's ever happened to me. I'm not completely at fault, but I should have... I don't know... handled it differently."

"Ah. I guess I shouldn't ask for details, then."

"I'm in love with her."

"Really?" Mom said sarcastically. "You don't say? That's only been coming for about twenty years."

"Mom. Stop."

"Oh, for goodness sake, Gavin. How could you not know? The two of you have been headed for this for a very long time. So what happened?"

"The distance. We're in two very different places."

"So move."

He wasn't sure he heard her correctly. His mother didn't want him working an hour away, but she was telling him to move? And what kind of move was she talking about?

"One of you has to. And I'm not talking geography. You have to take a chance. This is not safe territory. You're operating without a net, so to speak."

"I don't know what to do, Mom. I want to be with her. Marry her. Make a family."

"But…" Mom wasn't hanging on any formality.

"But I want to do it here. Or close to here, so my kids can have the same security I did growing up. Part of me thinks I should make that bold move, but there's another part of me that believes in deep roots."

"And Ally doesn't agree?" His mother took a sip of her coffee, her eyes never wavering.

"I don't know."

Silence. This was one of those moments where he wished he hadn't said anything because he was being judged. His mother didn't have to say a single word to let him know he'd fucked up royally.

"I should have talked to her more. I know."

"If you know, then why didn't you? Isn't this the same thing that happened last time?"

"Because she wasn't talking either," he said. "It's not just me. What if she doesn't want me in that life? You should have seen her, Mom. Smart, confident, she had total control of the event, of the people. She's amazing. Maybe I just don't fit with her life. Maybe that's why the discussion was so one sided."

"That's nonsense, and you know it. Good grief. I've never seen two people have more trouble getting out of their own way than the two of you. Do you love her?"

"With all my heart."

"And she loves you." His mother was breaking the problem down to its most basic.

"She said she did." Hearing her say it made him happy in ways he didn't think possible.

His mother's voice softened. "Did you tell her how you felt?"

"No. I didn't."

She was quiet for a moment. Eyes lowered, lips pursed. "I vowed from the second I became a mother that I would not strike one of my children, but so help me Gavin, I want to box your ears."

"Mom…"

"No. Don't *mom* me. You have some explaining to do, Doctor. And not to me."

He did. He had to find her and get her to forgive his stupidity. Saying it all out loud made his path clear as day. And it showed him once again how much he didn't deserve her. "I'm going to get some sleep. Then I'll head home, figure it out."

"So you just came to eat, or to get some sense kicked into you."

Gavin smiled as he kissed the top of his mother's head. "Probably a little of both, Ma."

"Good boy. I'll wake you up later and give you a hard

time. Then we can head to church."

He smiled. "I can't wait."

THERE WAS NO reason for Ally to stay at the ranch with Gavin gone, so she saw her friends the next morning, and then headed out towards home. Home being in Marietta, not Seattle.

That should have been her first clue that her time with him had changed everything.

Pulling up to the house, her parents were sitting on the front porch chatting with the neighbors next door. It was a typical Sunday morning in town. People were out for walks, happy to be done with the long winter. Gardens were being tended, and there was lots of traffic around the local churches. Small town life.

Simple. Honest. Loving.

Her mother rose from her chair when Ally's pulled in the driveway, the look on her face a mix of curiosity and concern. Maybe she should have gone back to Seattle to avoid all the questions, but as she discovered, avoidance wasn't her style.

She was, however, a "curl into a ball under the covers" kind of girl. She planned on doing that for at least a few days.

"Hey, sweetie." Her mother reached out and embraced her. "I saw Christine this morning at mass. She told me you and Gavin had a falling out."

"Wow, he didn't waste any time calling his family."

"Oh, he didn't call. He arrived at their farm about five-thirty this morning. Drove all night. Plans on staying another day or so."

What do you know? He'd done the same thing she'd done. He'd gone home. Not the home he'd made by himself, but the home where they had met and fallen in love, where their families were and hopefully where they would raise a family of their own.

Suddenly, Ally felt lighter. More hopeful. Maybe she could fix this without having to stake out his apartment or faking an illness at his hospital. Maybe she could just tell him what she was feeling, that she loved him, and all she wanted was to be with him, wherever that was.

Would that be enough?

Her heart was all she had to offer. It wasn't perfect. It made mistakes, but it was the best thing she had. And her heart loved him. If she were honest with herself, Ally would admit that she'd loved Gavin Clark since he beat up a bully in her defense decades ago.

Decades. And she'd ruined it in minutes.

He had always been her knight in shining armor, her partner in crime, her confidant and her best friend. They were meant to be together, he was her perfect match, and Ally was convinced that both of them coming straight back to Marietta was a sign that they were supposed to work it out.

They had to work it out.

Handing her mother the bag she'd tossed over her shoulder, Ally planted a kiss on Mom's cheek, and hugged her dad. These people had been her example growing up, loving each other no matter what was thrown their way.

She probably should wash off the car ride, but all she wanted was to see Gavin, to feel his arms around her, hear his deep voice, lose herself in his kiss.

There was no time to wait. "I'll be back in a little while."

"Where are you going?" Mom asked, grinning, already knowing the answer.

"To get my happy ever after." She hugged her parents. "I think it's my turn, don't you?"

"Absolutely." Her mother nodded, smiled, and shooed her towards her car.

This ride to Gavin was about trust. About letting someone else into her life. To relinquishing some control.

All she wanted was for him to forgive her.

For years, Ally had been all about controlling her future. And now she was going to do it again, and the stakes were higher than ever before. She just hoped she could get Gavin to forgive her, because without him, nothing else really mattered.

Chapter Eleven

T HERE WAS NOTHING quite like sleeping the day away—when you're twenty. When you're thirty-one, you feel like shit, and you have the knowledge you aren't falling asleep anytime soon.

Moving through the big house, Gavin had to smile at everything going on. Even on a Sunday, everyone was busy with something. His mother was in her sitting room reading a book, and his brothers were outside around the firepit, having beers together. It was a family day at home.

He found his father in the barn, checking on his favorite new foal. The male Quarter horse was already proving to be a handful, but he was going to be one of the crowning glories of the breeding program.

"How's he doing?" Gavin asked as he approached the stall.

"Very well. Getting big. We're trying to think of a name that suits. No luck so far."

Gavin nodded and watched the foal and his mother interact. Every time the baby did something his mother didn't like, she gently corrected him. It seemed the horse knew how to handle kids better than that mother at the wedding.

"Mom thinks I'm an idiot."

"If this has to do with Ally, I'd have to agree."

"Thanks for the support, Dad."

"Do you want me to soften it up, Gavin? Chew your food for you, so it's not too hard to swallow?"

"That's not funny."

His father pushed his hat back on his head. "No, son, it's not. Be a man. Stop trying to blame everyone else for your mistake. And losing that girl would be a mistake."

"I know. Believe me," Gavin said. "I know."

"That's all well and good, but what are you gonna do about it, son?"

"Hope she forgives me." It was possible she wouldn't, and although Gavin didn't want to think about it, it was a truth he couldn't avoid. "Beg, maybe."

"I have a feeling she will," his father said. "But you better think up some real pretty words for that apology."

"Yeah. I also need a plane ticket."

His father hooked the safety netting across the stall opening. "Why?"

"Why what?" There were a lot of questions on the table, Dad needed to be specific.

"Where are you going?"

"Seattle."

His father nodded, mopping the sweat from his forehead. "Okay, but before you go, you have company." His father nodded his head toward the big field. There, sitting on an old swing that was hung in an ancient oak tree was Ally. Her back was to him, and for the life of him, he had no idea what to do.

"How long has she been here?" he asked.

His father glanced at his watch. "Oh, over an hour."

An hour? "You could have woken me up."

"Nah. Ally said to let you sleep. Your mother offered to feed her, but she just wanted to sit on that old swing."

Of course she would. It was their special spot. When she'd come out to the farm, they'd head out to the field and Gavin would gently push her on the swing while they talked. It would go on for hours sometimes, but it never felt like it. The time they were together always went too fast.

He was at the final turning point with her. It was today or—

He left his father and walked out there, thinking about what the hell he was going to say. Why had she come?

Getting to her felt like it took forever, and a thousand possibilities ran through his mind. The sun was bright across the field dotted with daffodils signaling that winter was really over, and Ally seemed almost luminescent in the glow.

Once he reached her, he had to hold back and not just haul her into his arms and kiss her senseless. There was no telling what she wanted or how this was going to go.

Stepping up behind her, she turned her head, just in time to see him place his hands on her back, and give her a gentle push. "Hey."

"Hey," she said. "Have a good sleep?"

"Nah. Not really." *You weren't there*, he thought.

"Me either. I slept horribly."

"You left the ranch this morning?" he asked.

"Yeah. About nine o'clock. I almost drove to Bozeman to see you."

"Really? How would you have found me?"

A watery laugh escaped. "I was going to stake out the hospital. I was fully prepared to live on vending machine coffee and granola bars."

He laughed. The sweetness and sincerity of her confession struck a clean blow to his heart.

"I owe you an apology," she whispered. "I'm so sorry. I never should have been so cold and callous to you."

"No, I… it's okay. We've both made mistakes."

"I never meant to hurt you. I-I love you, Gavin, and…"

Her breath hitched, and before any more tears fell, Gavin walked around the swing and pulled her into his arms. He held her still, the sweet sobs coming quietly. "I love you, Ally. Please don't cry."

"Oh, God. I don't want to lose you. I don't. I didn't mean to be so hard and insensitive. I want us to have a life together."

"You do?" he asked.

"I do. It's all I want."

"Thank God."

She nodded against his chest. "Please don't let me make a stupid mistake again. I didn't listen to you when we were teenagers and I lost you for so long. I can't lose you again. I just can't."

Her tears were soaking his shirt while he held her tight. "I won't let you make a stupid mistake. I'll move to Seattle if you want. I'll go anywhere. As long as we're together, we're going to be all right."

Ally looked up. Her eyes were red from crying, her face streaked with tears, but no one had ever been as beautiful. She loved him, and Gavin had never been so relieved or happy.

"The city isn't for you, so instead I'm coming home. I can work here, grow my business if that's what I want to do. But what I want most in the world is to have my happy ever after with you. Only with you."

"My mission in life is to make you happy. I won't let you down."

"You never have. Never." Her arms slipped around his waist and she held him tight. "Can you work here? Or do you want to go someplace else?"

"Here is good. We'll work it out. We will always work things out." Taking her face in his hands, Gavin kissed each cheek, then dropped a kiss on her soft lips. "I love you, Allison Beaumont. I want to make a life with you, grow old with you. Marry me?"

She nodded, the tears coming faster and faster. "Yes. I

will."

Holding Ally close, Gavin's heart felt right again. It hadn't been that way since she'd left all those years ago.

"How many babies do you want?" she asked.

"As many as you want. I mean that. You want six, you can have six. We can build a house here on the farm, or in town closer to your folks."

"Will there be a swing and a gazebo?" she asked sweetly.

Not thinking he could be any more affected, Gavin's heart just about exploded. "Anything you want."

Finally, through her tears, a smile broke. Wide and beaming, there was nothing in the world like it. Ally put her hands on his shoulders and stretched up to kiss him. Then she kissed him again and again.

"You're my best thing, Gavin Clark. You make me a better person. I can't wait to start our lives together."

"I think we're a good team. I love you. You've always been my girl. Always."

"I love you, Gavin. I have since I was nine years old."

"Well," he said, kissing her soundly. "It took you long enough to tell me."

Epilogue

Thanksgiving Eve

TRUE TO FORM, Marietta would have a snowy Thanksgiving, ushering in the holiday season right on schedule. As the snow fell that afternoon, all Gavin hoped was that the bad roads didn't keep him from getting home. They hadn't. He'd been late to supper, but he'd made it.

Ally was already in the house they'd rented in town a few months ago, arriving from a Key West destination wedding the day before. But tonight, before making love to his beautiful fiancée, Gavin was going to see the boys for the first time in over six months.

The auction in the spring had changed the all their lives. None of them could have predicted that with a winning bid came love. Every one of them had fallen hard. For a bunch of tough guys, they were putty in the hands of their women.

Walking into Grey's Saloon, Gavin fondly remembered the night Ally dropped so much money to secure a wedding date.

Now he was planning on being her wedding date for as long as they both lived. After months of bouncing between cities and their hometown, he bought her a ring and he planned on giving it to her on Thanksgiving. It was fitting, since she was the thing in his life for which he was most thankful.

"At least it didn't snow too hard. Worst case, we could crash at your new place if it's too tough to get home." Colt Ewing slapped Gavin on the back, then gave him a hearty hug. "It's good to see you, man. It feels like it's been forever since we were up on that stage."

Gavin bear-hugged his friend and said, "I know what you mean. Six months ago we were bachelors, every one of us." From where he was sitting at the round table in the center of the room, Gavin could see the door. As if on cue, both Nick and Code walked in; both of them had been traveling with their fiancées, and to be honest, he'd never seen either of his high-octane friends so relaxed.

"Cassidy and Hayley were yacking up a storm at the house. Where are Talon and Ally?" Nick straddled a chair and grabbed one of the beers Gavin had ordered from the middle of the table.

"Talon is with Parker." Colt replied. "They're making pies for tomorrow."

"Ally's at the new house. She's unpacking. Just got home from an event." Gavin couldn't wait to see her.

"I've been given instructions," Code said, as he pulled a folded piece of paper from his pocket. All at once, laughter erupted from the table. "Hayley has questions."

"Have your marching orders, do you, pussycat?" Colt couldn't resist a good ribbing.

"Fuck off," Code said. "Like you don't bend over backwards for Talon?"

"I didn't say that. What does Hayley want to know?"

Gavin held in his laughter, to his own amazement. Of all of them, Code was the most no-nonsense. He hadn't had an easy life, and he deserved to be happy. They all did.

"Hayley and I want to set a wedding date. She's requested information about your weddings, so there're no conflicts." Turning to Gavin, he said, "She also wants you to ask Ally if she'll be the event planner."

He knew Ally would jump at the chance to plan Code and Hayley's wedding. To her, nothing was better than helping a couple plan the perfect day. That they were all friends was even better.

Business out of the way, they talked about jobs and sports, how their favorite teams had been losing, and during the conversation what Gavin noticed was that all the guys, him included, were settled, less on edge. They'd all been at loose ends, one way or another, when they walked into that auction, and now they had futures that would include women who loved them, kids… a place to call home.

Maybe this was Karma. None of them had wanted to get up on that stage. There were a thousand reasons to say no. Each of them could have put up the money needed to build the helipad—but by going the extra mile, the payoff had been huge. Sure, the town got what it needed, and Gavin never doubted that it would; but he and the boys got what they needed too, and that was completely unexpected.

Gavin rose from his chair, anxious to get home to his bride-to-be. Downing his beer, he hugged the men who were like brothers to him.

"Come out to the ranch for dessert tomorrow night. Mom likes nothing better than to feed you hoodlums. Bring the girls, and Parker."

There was no doubt they would all be there. They always were.

Walking out onto the snowy street, Gavin looked around, happy to be home. From where he stood, he could see the lights from their tiny house on the hill just beyond the row of stores. Ally was there waiting for him.

His phone chirped and he checked to see a text from her. *Hurry home. I miss you.*

Home. All of them had a new appreciation for what it meant. They might not all settle in Marietta, but they had all found their place and someone to love them.

Gavin smiled and looked at the house again.

For him home was where Ally was. It was that simple.

On my way, he sent back, and he headed up the hill.

The End

Acknowledgements

I've absolutely loved taking this amazing trip to Marietta, Montana where love always wins. *Weekend With Her Bachelor* was so much fun to write, and I hope you enjoy reading Gavin and Ally's story as much as I loved telling it.

The idea of a friends to lover's story, coupled with a reunion, gave me a rich place to start. Add four lifelong friends, close-knit families and a bachelor auction in this lively small town, and sparks will fly.

No story is ever written in isolation, and I am honored to have shared this series with three amazing authors. Charlene Sands, Robin Bielman and Sinclair Jayne, we make a great team, and I'm so happy we were able to revisit the Bachelor Auction together.

I need to say thanks to all the people who helped this book come alive. My local RWA chapter, the Long Island Romance Writers, continue to provide inspiration and support. (A few of you lent your names to this story, so I thank you all for permission.)

Many thanks to the amazing Tule Team—Lindsey, Meghan and Danielle; you ladies are priceless. As always, I thank the amazing Jane Porter for inviting me into the Tule family. Tule is my mothership, and I thank you, and the founding authors, for creating a place for writers to spread their wings. Endless appreciation to my editor Laurie Johnson, who helped bring the story into focus, and my copy editor and friend, Jennifer Gracen who polished up a very messy manuscript.

My family? They put up with me, they feed me when I'm on deadline, and they love me when I am at my least loveable. For that I am forever grateful. Love you. xo

Thank you for joining me on this wonderful ride. Please stay in touch! You can email me, or find my social media hangouts at my website jeanniemoon.com.

Love to all,
Jeannie

The Bachelor Auction Returns

Bachelor for Hire by Charlene Sands
Falling for Her Bachelor by Robin Bielman
Seducing the Bachelor by Sinclair Jayne
Weekend with Her Bachelor by Jeannie Moon

For more stories from The Bachelor Auction, check out...

The Bachelor Auction Series

Bound to the Bachelor by Sarah Mayberry
Bachelor at Her Bidding by Kate Hardy
The Bachelor's Baby by Dani Collins
What a Bachelor Needs by Kelly Hunter
In Bed with the Bachelor by Megan Crane
One Night with Her Bachelor by Kat Latham

Available now at your favorite online retailer!

About the Author

Jeannie Moon has always been a romantic. When she's not spinning tales of her own, Jeannie works as a school librarian, thankful she has a job that allows her to immerse herself in books and call it work. Married to her high school sweetheart, Jeannie has three kids, three lovable dogs and a mischievous cat and lives in her hometown on Long Island, NY. If she's more than ten miles away from salt water for any longer than a week, she gets twitchy.

Visit Jeannie's website at www.jeanniemoon.com

Thank you for reading

Weekend with Her Bachelor

If you enjoyed this book, you can find more from all our great authors at TulePublishing.com, or from your favorite online retailer.

TULE
PUBLISHING

Printed in Great Britain
by Amazon

17583562R00099